DC
VENGE

DOCTOR WHO
VENGEANCE ON VAROS

Based on the BBC television series by Philip Martin by
arrangement with BBC Books, a division of BBC
Enterprises Ltd

PHILIP MARTIN

Number 106 in the
Doctor Who Library

A TARGET BOOK
published by
the Paperback Division of
W.H. Allen & Co. Plc

A Target Book
Published in 1988
By the Paperback Division of
W.H. Allen & Co. Plc
44 Hill Street, London W1X 8LB

First published in Great Britain by
W.H. Allen & Co. Plc 1988

The BBC producer of *Vengeance on Varos* was John Nathan-Turner
The director was Ron Jones
The role of the Doctor was played by Colin Baker

Typeset by Phoenix Photosetting, Chatham

Printed and bound in Great Britain by
Cox & Wyman Ltd, Reading

ISBN 0 426 20291 0

Contents

The Dome of Death

The Random Laser Beam Emitter turned ominously on its axis, clicked, as if in irritation, then spat a searing beam of force at the lean young man chained to a wall in a corridor deep within the main Punishment Dome of the former prison planet of Varos.

Desperately twisting in the chains, Jondar succeeded in evading the laser beam; but the heat of its passing scalded skin stretched taut across his left side, causing a howl of anguish to be torn from lips parched by the tension of his long ordeal.

In the ceiling of the corridor a television camera monitored each movement of the terrified prisoner below, beaming every detail of his suffering into the home-cells of the viewers, for whom the ruling officer class of Varos termed this 'entertainment' and 'instruction'.

In the communications section of the Media Dome a young technician, Bax, wearing the orange uniform of Comm Tech Division, concentrated on the bank of monitors before him. Many screens revealed the plight of other unfortunates in different sectors of the Punishment Dome. Bax, whose job it was to select the most dramatic pictures to broadcast to the viewers of Varos, had a hunch that Jondar's luck at dodging the Random Laser Beams could not last much longer. Delicately he adjusted a focal control, bringing into close-up the rebel's haggard face with its lines of tension and fear.

Impassively, Bax watched Jondar trying to muster his resources to evade the next deadly beam that would soon radiate toward him.

The home-cell unit of Etta and her husband, Arak, was of the standard size for two Varosians without children. It comprised a bedroom just large enough to contain a two-tiered bunk and a living room with a plasti-table and two tubular metal chairs that faced a viewing screen which occupied the entire area of one wall.

Before this screen sat Etta, closely observing the harrowing pictures transmitted from the interior of the Punishment Dome. Beside her, on a specially fitted wire arm rest installed courtesy of View Data Division, lay her meticulously compiled viewer's report on which she noted down not only her own reactions to the television output but also the occasionally biting comments of her husband, Arak.

As the camera adjustment changed to a close-up of the sweating, begrimed features of Jondar, Etta dutifully noted the time and the altered angle, then glanced up as Arak entered, tired and exhausted from long hours spent working for his detachment of the Mining Corps. Wearily, Arak removed his protective helmet and surveyed the room until finally his red-rimmed eyes rested reluctantly on the image of Jondar that filled the screen and dominated the room.

'Not him again!'

'Yeh. He's still on. Still alive – just.' A movement on the screen brought Etta's attention back to Jondar who appeared to be bracing himself to face another bolt of destruction.

Arak pursed his lips in a small grimace of scorn. 'Comm Div must be runnin' short of rebos to laser-ise; he was on before I went out to work this mornin'.'

Etta's concentration was now back onto the wall screen. 'He's survived all day. Almost a record.'

'Huh.' Arak unzipped the jacket of his black overalls. 'Probably all fake anyhow.' Etta snorted in disagreement as he knew she would. Arak resented the seriousness with which his wife treated her viewer's reports, although he accepted gratefully the extra credits that supplemented his meagre wages as a worker in the Zeiton Ore division of Mine Tech.

'Anything to eat?' he asked, wearily turning away from the seemingly all-pervasive image of Jondar's fear radiating from the screen. Etta made no reply. 'My ration, where is it?'

Etta, absorbed in the quick cutting of camera angles between the clicking Random Laser Beam Emitter and the growing consternation of Jondar, jabbed a finger in the general direction of their food locker.

Arak sighed, trying to remember a time when his wife would serve food to him. Before viewer's reports, he decided, though not before compulsory television. Arak could not recall a time when the wall screen had not been a constant companion to his home life.

'I'll get it myself then.' His voice with its hint of reproach goaded Etta instantly.

'Do that and shut up while you're about it!'

As Arak rummaged about in the almost empty food locker Etta leaned forward in her chair. Tensely she took up her view data pen and prepared to record every last detail of the rebel Jondar's death.

The beam would strike where? Jondar desperately calculated the odds against a laser beam streaming towards his left-hand side for a third consecutive time. Almost too tired to decide anything on a logical basis any more, he fought back a desire to slump and surrender to a moment of searing pain followed by sweet oblivion. Resolutely he gazed into the revolving chamber of the Laser Beam Emitter that stood opposite him. The chamber slowed; the clicking of its random aim programme completed its cycle. Jondar gambled on another left-side beam and hurled himself to the right. The metal chains restrained him cruelly but the bolt of force bored into the pitted rock behind, hardly causing him anything more than a painful memory of previous more narrow escapes.

Sobbing with relief Jondar slumped down, head hanging, heart jumping with gratitude for being allowed to live for a few precious minutes more.

'Those chains are too slack,' a voice rasped behind Bax. Startled, the technician turned to see the battered features of the Chief Officer staring at Jondar on the main screen.

'Yes, Chief, they must be.'

'See they're tightened. We mustn't bore our audience. Survival has its interest only for a limited term of viewer attention. They must see the rebel obliterated soon. See to it.'

'Yes, Chief.' Bax saluted the all-powerful Chief Officer.

'But adjust the chain off-camera. There's notice of a vote-in later tonight, isn't there?'

Bax checked his programme sheet.

'Report of the negotiations between the Governor and the Galatron Mining Corporation?'

'That's it. Do it then so the viewers won't know why Jondar's luck has run out so abruptly.'

The Chief turned away, the screens' blue light reflecting from the skin of his completely shaven skull. Bax watched him go. Although he believed Jondar deserving of death he disliked shortening the chains and the odds against the rebel's life, but trained to obey, he reached for the microphone switch that would connect him to the guards' HQ within the Punishment Dome.

'Prisoner survived. Equals previous best time of escaping obliteration.' Etta neatly completed the sentence as Arak angrily contemplated a small can without a label or anything else that might indicate what kind of food it contained.

'Is this all there is?' Arak tossed the can to Etta who caught it neatly.

'Only workfeed I could get.'

Arak snorted in derision. 'It wouldn't fill a clinker mole's belly let alone a working man's.'

His wife shrugged. 'It's the shortages. Maybe the Governor will explain; there's to be a punch-in vote tonight.'

For Arak this was the final irritation of the day. 'Voting, voting. This Governor calls a punch-in vote every time he wants to change his trousers . . . gimme . . !'

Etta handed the can back to Arak without immediate comment but, being a supporter of the present Governor, she was unable to resist asking 'What will the next Governor do better?'

Struggling to open the workfeed tin, Arak only muttered, 'Everything . . . anything . . .'

The top of the can finally gave under pressure, peeling back to reveal a dark mass of protein, the origin of which was not easily identifiable.

'Ugh! What is this supposed to be, Etta?'

'Her at food-dole couldn't say. Seems factory ran out of labels.'

Arak lifted the tin nearer to his nostrils.

'Cor . . . I can't eat this . . . it smells like the leavings of a sand slug.'

Etta stood up, her hand eagerly reaching out for the tin of food.

5

Arak, pleased that at last he could thwart his wife in some little thing, grinned back at her.

'I'll keep it to chuck at the screen when your beloved Governor comes on beggin' my vote!'

Etta regarded her husband with an expression of prim reproof.

'Attacking Comm Tech property can bring loss of viewing rights. Way you're thinking, Arak, you'll soon be in that one's place . . .' With a jerk of her head, Etta directed Arak's attention towards Jondar who was still slumped with exhaustion in his chains. Seeing her husband's tremor of fear Etta continued, 'Like to see how long *you'd* last in the Dome; not even survive the first mind-distort test, you.'

'Living with you, Etta, prepares me to put up with anything.'

Suddenly the wall screen became blank. Disconcerted, both of them waited for the familiar logo of Comm Tech to appear. When it did they both relaxed, feeling somehow that everything was all right in their world once again. From the wall speaker the gloomy national anthem of Varos began its slow military march. Arak knew what that meant: a broadcast by the Governor with a compulsory vote to follow.

Without quite understanding why, Arak began to rail at the wall screen with its huge stylised letter 'V' that dominated their cell-like room.

'Why have they stopped sending pictures from the Dome? Pathetic; when did they last show something worth watching? When did we last see a decent execution!'

'Last week,' said Etta, evenly.

'No.'

'Yes,' Etta insisted, 'the blind man.'

'That was a repeat.'

'It wasn't. You're thinking of that infiltrator; and he wasn't blind, not at the beginning . . .'

6

Arak yawned. 'Yes, he was . . . anyway . . . I'm tired, think I'll go to my bunk.'

'You can't do that,' Etta said as she reached for a metal box placed beneath her chair and started to remove two voting transmitter units, one marked *Yes* and the other *No*. 'You can't go to sleep yet: we got to vote later.'

'Do it for me,' Arak yawned again. Horrified, Etta turned from the voting transmitters.

'You want Pol Corps calling here? Do you, Arak?'

Amused by his wife's obvious fear, Arak smiled easily. 'How could they know it wasn't me voting, eh?'

Etta's reply slackened the grin on Arak's mouth. 'I'd tell them,' she said with a determination that Arak found quite chilling.

The TARDIS, in a limbo of time and space, was without movement. Inside the console room the Doctor hunched down beside a roundel, his arm immersed in a serpent's nest of multi-coloured wirings. With a sudden flourish he extricated his arm, slammed the roundel shut, stood up, and with a shout of triumph addressed the patiently waiting Peri.

'That's it!'

Unimpressed, Peri regarded the Doctor dourly.

'I don't believe it.'

'How can you? I haven't told you what it is I've done!'

Worriedly, Peri took a backward step.

'You sound too confident. I really don't think I want to know.'

'What? Why?' The Doctor blinked in bewilderment.

'Every time you sound confident nowadays, Doctor, something awful seems to happen!'

Like what, the Doctor wondered, scratching his

head. Then for some reason he shouted at the startled girl, 'What *exactly* do you mean!'

Warily, Peri watched the Doctor. Since his recent regeneration the process of stabilisation of his personality seemed uneven, to say the least. With what she hoped sounded like sweet reason she recounted the incidents of their recent journey.

'Since we left Telos you've caused three electrical fires, a total power failure and a near collision with a storm of asteroids.'

'I've never said I was perfect,' the Doctor muttered sullenly.

'No,' sighed Peri. 'But before each and every accident you've said in a loud confident voice, "That's it!" And to be honest, Doc, I'm thinking more and more about returning to America to complete my studies.'

'Right – that's where you'll go!' The Doctor activated the TARDIS's controls and adjusted the co-ordinates to the twentieth century on Earth. A low hum came from the TARDIS as the central rotor started to oscillate.

Peri frowned angrily; she hadn't expected her threat to be translated into such instant action.

'Oh, you're the most inconsistent and intolerant man I've ever met.'

Intent on steering the TARDIS, the Doctor pondered the accusation before exploding with a squall of indignation: 'Intolerant, *me*? *Intolerant.*'

Peri backed away. 'Why are you shouting?'

'Because . . .' The Doctor paused, frowning at the rising column before him. '. . . because there's something wrong.'

'What?'

The Doctor cocked an ear first one way then the other.

'You look like a hound dog listening for its master, Doctor. Why? What's up?'

8

'Sshh . . . there's something amiss in the power units.'

'*Still*, after all the work you've done?'

The Doctor nodded sadly. 'It's in the one area I didn't check . . .'

'Oh, great. But aren't there emergency circuits or something?'

Preoccupied, the Doctor checked a dial worriedly. 'Yes . . . but it seems as if that function is about to become defunct too . . .'

Peri refused to believe that the situation could be as serious as the Doctor's anxious pose would indicate.

'You can do something, Doc, I'm sure.'

The Doctor scanned the warning instruments that flashed and blinked before him. Finally he nodded sagely.

'I know what this is, Peri.'

'What?'

'A conundrum wrapped in a dilemma.'

'What does that mean?' asked Peri in bewilderment.

'Oh, just that we may well be marooned within this pocket of space.'

'For how long?' Peri said, expecting an hour at best, a day at worst. But the Doctor spread his hands in a hopeless resigned gesture and said with utter certainty:

'Evermore.'

2

The Vital Vote

Alone in his office the Governor wondered how many more days he might survive as ruler of Varos, given that the rules of the constitution demanded that he die once his popularity with his television audience had faded.

The Governor's head, with its mane of yellow hair, sagged against the back of his chair in an apathy of despair. Above him the screen of the Human Cell Disintegrator reflected dully the lights of the office. The Governor knew how quickly the HCD device could activate and pour down rays of pain and destruction if the people of Varos voted against him; alternatively, when they balloted in his favour warm golden rays cascaded down, bringing energy, optimism and new determination to govern wisely.

Now the Governor was exhausted after surviving a sequence of three losing vote-ins. He wondered how he could find the strength to carry on battling for a fair price on the sale of the mineral known as Zeiton-7.

Into his office, carried by two burly black-helmeted bodyguards, came the negotiator of Galatron Consolidated, the alien Sil from the planet Thoros-Beta, fresh from his mud bath and eager to resume discussion.

Wearily, the Governor hauled himself upright and bowed to his opponent who raised a claw in indifferent acknowledgement.

Leaf-green in colour and perched in his water tank, Sil was a member of a species of mutant amphibians whose cunning intelligence was hampered by an immobile body that required frequent watering in order to breathe. The features of Sil's pug face were now clenched angrily, and the scaly crescent that ran from between his rheumy eyes to the back of his head bristled with impatience as he glared up at the Governor.

'You a reasonable man are,' the faulty translational voice box slung on his plated chest crackled out. 'Lower the price of your Zeiton ore!'

'My people deserve a fair rate for their labour,' the Governor replied with icy politeness.

'Who else will buy from you if my corporation withdraws its contract? You are not a rich planet; Zeiton is all you have to sell.'

It was the truth. There had been some success in exporting to other worlds video recordings of the grisly happenings within the Punishment Dome but not enough sales to replace the loss of such a vital market as that for Zeiton-7. Both negotiators looked impassively at each other. The Governor decided to bluff it out.

'Then we will have to sell elsewhere.'

A cackle of laughter burst from Sil's mouth. Its eerie sound brought in the Chief Officer from the adjoining communications centre.

'You are agreed then,' he started.

'*No!*' Sil's laughter became an abrupt squeal of anger. 'No, no . . . *no*! My patience exhausted is!'

The Chief addressed the Governor politely and firmly: 'The people are anxious for a decision on the new price of our product, sir.'

Impatiently, the Governor took a step away. 'Delay my broadcast.'

As custodian of the constitution of Varos the Chief Officer held a unique position. In some respects he had greater power than the Governor himself. Sensing this, Sil addressed the Chief in a voice of pained sincerity.

11

'Already I have beyonded my authority to please this Governor.'

'We must have an increase,' the Governor said stubbornly. 'Your company pays us hardly enough to exist.'

The slug-like Sil settled back into his water tank complacently. 'We pay ample.' He said and waved his bearers to carry him out of the Governor's presence.

Outside the Governor's office Sil and the Chief Officer glanced warily about them, making sure no one could overhear their conversation.

Sil began the exchange. 'Like this present Governor we do not. Replace you must arrange most soon.'

'My dear Sil, a little patience is all that is required. Trust me,' the Chief Officer said soothingly.

'Maybe I should dispense with your pay-offs, offer that and you as a bribe to him?' Sil's eyes glinted with calculation.

'You really mustn't threaten me . . .' the Chief Officer began but was distracted by the sudden glowing of a red light above the door of the Governor's office.

'Enough talk . . .' Sil motioned to his bearers. 'I wish to witness the last suffering moments of this fool governorship.'

Moving towards the bank of monitors Sil and the Chief began to watch what seemed certain to be the final broadcast of the present Governor.

When Peri returned to the console room she found the Doctor had not stirred from his position propped up against a wall of the stationary TARDIS. Peri ran her fingers through the 726 pages of the bulky manual marked '*TARDIS – Service*'. 'Here . . .' she said and thrust the thick volume at the Doctor who glanced at the title then pushed it listlessly aside.

'Doctor, won't that tell us what's wrong with the TARDIS?'

'I know exactly what category of disaster has befallen us, thank you.'

'The comparator?'

'Not this time.' The Doctor reached for the manual. 'If you insist, I may as well confirm my diagnosis.' Ruefully, he tested the weight of the technical volume. 'Be something to pass eternity with, I suppose.' And with that, to Peri's surprise, he began to pore over its contents.

Throughout the Governor's careful summary of the stalled negotiations with Sil, Arak and Etta had never taken their eyes from the wall video screen. Now nearing the end of his address the Governor leant forward and spoke with hardly a trace of emotion in his voice, as if he was merely wishing the population of Varos a pleasant National Pardon Day.

'Viewers of Varos, I ask that we agree to hold out for a fair price for our Zeiton ore. Those in favour vote "yes" for a ten per cent reduction in our food supplies. Those who wish for full bellies today and nothing to eat tomorrow can, of course, punch their *No* button.'

'Right!' Arak was up on his feet and heading for the voting boxes before Etta could start to reason with him.

'Arak!' was all she managed to say before he plunged down the *No* switch. Glowering at her husband, Etta crossed to the TV controls and pressed *Yes* in direct retaliation.

The visual display unit linked to the HCD device showed the voting totals: 633,156 *Yes*, 987,627 *No*.

Bracing himself, and still on camera, the Governor bravely placed his arms along the supports of his chair.

Restraining clamps held his legs while steel bands snapped around his wrists. The pain, when it

13

descended on him, was devastating. Its shock permeated every cell in his wracked body, tormenting, destroying.

The office faded. For the Governor there was no other world but the dreadful pain and misery inflicted by the Cell Disintegrator. It could be so easy, he thought, to allow his life and the troubles of Varos to slip away; but on the edge of oblivion the HCD ceased its downpour of destruction. Dimly the Governor felt a faint pulse still beating in his veins. Almost dispassionately he wondered whether it would strengthen or fall away into the nothingness of death.

Tears started in Etta's eyes as she viewed the crumpled figure of the seemingly dead Governor lying inert in his chair. Beside her, Arak gloated at the video wall screen.

'Dead at last. Let's hope the hazard throws up someone better able to feed us next time.'

'Shut up!' Etta's anger spilled over but, about to upbraid her husband, she caught a stirring on the large wall screen, a movement that quelled her anger instantly.

'He lives!' She threw out an exultant arm as on the screen the debilitated Governor regained consciousness and feebly gestured for help from unseen assistants.

'He's survived!' Etta clapped her hands in wonder, 'Four losing votes, almost a record.'

'Huh!' Arak scowled first at his wife then at the screen. 'Not for long. The next vote will do him in for sure.'

In the TARDIS the Doctor was suddenly animated by hope. Peri watched the transformation with amazement as he busily referred to the service manual and checked actual readings against manual power ratio tables.

Then, with an impatient chiding gesture, he thrust the manual into Peri's hands and began to try to revive the stationary TARDIS. Suddenly the rotor column moved and lifted.

'Doctor!' Peri began excitedly.

'Yes. Yes, it moved. I've managed to activate some emergency power source.'

'That's wonderful!'

'We've enough for a limited flight, no more. The transitional elements have lost their capacity to generate orbital energy. They must be replaced.'

'How long would that take?'

'No time at all,' the Doctor paused. 'It's not the fitting that's the problem. We must reline the trans-power system with a mineral called Zeiton-7. It's to be found on only one planet that I know of.' Peri couldn't understand the Doctor's troubled expression.

'Let's make for there then,' she said impatiently.

The Doctor considered the possibilities open to them. Thinking aloud, he circled the driving column of the TARDIS.

'If we use the emergency power unit, we might just reach the planet of Varos during their mining era . . .'

'Let's do it then,' said Peri impatiently, 'Anything's better than being stuck here, watching each other wrinkle up with age!'

Pausing in his agitated pacing the Doctor's eyes rested on his companion.

'That shows you know nothing of Varos,' he said grimly but then, resignedly, he began to set the co-ordinates that might land them on the bleak, desolate world of Varos.

3

Execution!

Sil was hardly pleased. The transitional voice box on his green-plated chest bumped up and down as the Thoros-Betan stabbed an angry finger at the monitor screen. 'The Governor lives on . . . you . . . you . . . promised . . .' he spluttered. The Chief went to pat the glistening shoulder quivering below him, then changed his mind.

'Next time he will die,' he said soothingly.

'Next time should be now!' Sil broke off as the Governor appeared in the doorway of his office.

Wearily, as protocol demanded, he looked for permission to leave his domain from the Chief Officer. The Governor's dry, cracked lips formed the words but such was the state of his exhaustion after the ministrations of the Cell Disintegrator that the force of breath to carry his words would not come.

'Permission to leave granted, sir,' the Chief said authoritatively and helped the Governor to a stool which was hastily provided by the monitoring technician, Bax.

'Thank you. Thank . . . I feel . . .'

Sil calculatingly saw his chance and, wishing to gain advantage, took what he thought was a softened approach.

'Should we resume negotiations now, your Governorship?'

Sil's voice penetrated the Governor's hearing like the

16

squeal of chalk on blackboard. He looked askance at the Chief, appealing mutely for some time to recover but the Chief looked away as if unaware of the Governor's desperate need.

'My . . . my office . . .' the Governor said feebly, then tried to follow the alien negotiator but staggered and almost fell under the effort.

'Steady, sir.' Bax quickly offered a supporting arm.

'Thank you . . .' The sweat glistened on the Governor's drawn features.

'Sir, you need a respite to build up your strength,' advised Bax.

'Yes . . . but how? A Governor must govern.'

Bax hesitated but then plunged ahead with his suggestion.

'Why not give the people a bonus? An execution . . . Ask them to vote as to whether or not you should execute the rebel Jondar. It's a few weeks since an execution on video; they're bound to agree.'

The Governor glanced at the Chief for an opinion and, much as the Chief disliked the prospect of the Governor surviving even for an extra day, he grudgingly felt he had little option but to endorse the technician's suggestion.

'Good idea. I'll instigate the vote-in and arrange for Jondar's dispatch. What exactly had you in mind for the manner of his execution?'

The Governor groped for an answer. Again Bax, bright and eager, came up with a solution.

'The Random Laser Beam Emitter . . . can I suggest the rebel dies by means of a massive build-up of its power?'

The Chief frowned. 'We've never used anything like that.'

Bax, borne along by enthusiasm, plunged on excitedly. 'I've worked it all out. If you neutralise the Q-switch and build up a giant pulse of light, an explo-

17

sion of focused laser energy will wipe the prisoner out of existence!'

'Too quick. We wouldn't be able to sell videos of such an instant execution.'

Bax nodded, having already anticipated the Chief's objection.

'It's the uncertainty. No one knows quite when the power will blow. We could get ten minutes of tension out of the prisoner's apprehension, fear, terror.'

The Chief rubbed his chin thoughtfully, thinking of possible video sales on other worlds. 'It is novel, I suppose.'

'And the video, I'm sure . . .'

'Yes, yes.'

Turning to the Governor, Bax pressed home the logic of his idea: 'You said we must export or die.'

'Yes, I did.' The Governor, sick and weary, thought longingly of the life-enhancing rays that would pour down upon him if the people voted 'Yes' for Jondar's execution. The rebel had to die anyway. Why not this way, in the unusual manner that Bax proposed?

'Very well. Arrange it, Chief. I will ask the people for their verdict.'

The Chief saluted. Eager to activate a vote-in, Bax turned back to his monitors and control panel while the Governor started with faltering steps what seemed to him to be a long trek back to his domain. Half-way across the communications room he paused and turned to Bax who had just alerted the viewers of Varos to attend their screens.

'Thanks for the suggestion, Bax.'

'My pleasure, sir.' Bax next pressed the override button that allowed him into the communications system of the guards of the Punishment Dome.

'End random pulses. Conserve c/b, inform prison control centre, prepare viewer warnings of imminent public execution.'

18

With a judder and a jar the TARDIS tried to reach the time and destination decreed by her co-ordinates. Anxiously, the Doctor and Peri watched the driving column rise and fall, then hesitate and almost stop.

'Come on!' the Doctor urged. 'If we stop now Varos won't even have been colonised as a prison planet!'

As if responding to her master's voice the TARDIS found a last plunge of energy from her failing power circuits and teetered onwards towards the latter part of the twenty-third century and the mining era of the planet Varos.

Jondar raised his head as the words heralding his death were spoken over him.

'For sedition, thought-rebellion and incitement of others to unionise and terrorise, the vote of the people of Varos was for your death to take place by laser obliteration!'

Jondar tried to focus his thoughts. He heard the death sentence but the acute realisation of it was yet to sweep over him.

'The Governor was to consider my appeal for clemency . . .' he faltered.

'Our Governor bows to the will of his people.' The Chief turned slightly so that the watching camera could take in his left profile. He raised the proclamation document dramatically and spoke with ominous finality. 'As System Arbiter and Chief Officer I confirm that conditions of our constitution have been complied with. I therefore permit the execution to proceed.'

'When?' was all Jondar could say hopelessly.

'At eight o'clock. Prime viewing time. You have enough time to compose yourself.' The Chief paused slightly then added mockingly, 'All of five short minutes.'

All there was to do then was to flick the controlling

Q-switch on the RLBE and to withdraw with his guards. With a dramatic flourish, the Chief rolled up the proclamation and turned away from the laser grille that already was beginning to build up the power that, all too soon for Jondar, would bypass its control circuits and hurl a beam of such immense force that it would obliterate Jondar and drive far into the protective ceramic casing that protected the structure of the Punishment Dome.

Out of earshot of the microphones and with his back to the ever-watchful cameras above, the Chief took a young guard, Maldak, aside. 'It's not certain when obliteration will take place. Stay clear of the execution site. You have your anti-hallucination helmet?' Maldak nodded, hoping the nervousness he felt would not be apparent to such a powerful authority as the Chief. 'Switched on?'

'Yes, sir.'

'I wouldn't wish one of my guards to succumb to the phantoms of the Punishment Dome, not with all of Varos watching.'

'No, sir.'

'Good.' The Chief glanced back at the condemned man in his chains and the pulsing, throbbing Laser Obliteration Unit before him. Motioning his guards to him, the Chief and his cohorts withdrew, marching away with robot-like precision.

Left with the lone guard, Jondar could feel the last minutes of his life thudding away. The green pulse of the laser unit before him seemed to grow ever more intense, and now an accompanying ominous whine began to grow, the pitch of which seemed to echo around the chamber as if an elephant had been mortally wounded and had decided to share its death throes with the unfortunate Jondar.

To Maldak, too, the sound seemed as much to come from behind him as from the designated instrument of execution. Nervously he risked a glance behind and saw the blue blur of the TARDIS in its first stage of materialisation. What Maldak had feared had begun to come true. He reached upwards to check if the anti-hallucin switch was on. It was, but not working. Maldak decided he couldn't disgrace the corps of guards by succumbing to imaginary dangers, not with all of Varos watching. He decided to ignore the trumpetings and concentrate instead in seeing Jondar sent into oblivion.

In the home-cell of Etta and Arak there was great excitement. Etta was poised to report every movement of excited response from her husband as he watched the video screen intently. Arak stared, fascinated at Jondar on screen, while in the background of the shot a blue rectangular object appeared; but such was the anticipation in waiting for the massive laser beam to sear Jondar that Arak failed to notice it.

'Any moment now!' he said with relish. 'He won't dodge this one, that's for certain.'

'We're back in the Middle Ages, Doctor!' Peri gestured towards the TARDIS screen that showed the chained, half-naked figure of Jondar staring dully at the instrument of his imminent demise.

The Doctor checked the data of their position once again. 'No . . .' he said cheerily. 'For once we've made it to where we should be.'

'Look!' Peri pointed at the screen on which the figure of Maldak now loomed. The beam gun in the guard's hand was directed straight at them. The force beam streamed towards the screen then deflected harmlessly.

'Friendly of him,' the Doctor said mildly, then began to collate data on the outside environment.

Maldak could not believe that such a large object as the

21

TARDIS could be imaginary, but such were the tricks and sensory distortions that were deliberately engineered into the Punishment Dome that it was possible he might be making an utter fool of himself. Maldak decided to call his Control Centre for assistance.

'Report of fault on helmet hallucin-filter . . . permission to withdraw?' he spoke softly into the microphone that was another feature of his helmet.

'Stay until after obliteration.' The reply crackled back immediately from the Controller, Quillam.

There was nothing else to do but obey. Maldak turned his back on the now fully-materialised TARDIS and stoically composed himself to witness the scene of execution about to take place before him.

'Artificial atmosphere . . . enclosed . . . rock . . . underground . . . breathable . . .' Peri paused, not understanding the atmospheric details now appearing on the TARDIS VDU unit before her.

'What?' The Doctor leaned over her shoulder, scanning the data scrolling up on the screen. 'Distorted readings . . . must be . . . yes, carbon dioxide increasing . . . increasing . . . all the time. Peri, it must be from a nearby source . . .'

Peri looked up at the viewer screen, at the sickly green light that reflected from the strained features of Jondar.

'What is this place? Why did that guard fire at us then turn away as if we didn't exist?'

'Let's go and ask him, shall we?' the Doctor said simply and before Peri could say a word he was off towards the exit of the TARDIS. With a gulp of apprehension Peri made herself follow the Doctor.

With the moment of death approaching, Jondar stared at the grille, heard the power whine and growl like a predatory creature straining to be unleashed. Jondar thought of his woman, Areta, and hoped she wouldn't be watching his final moments on a screen somewhere; but if she was, at least he would die with as much bravery and dignity as he could muster.

Jondar straightened and stared defiantly at the Laser Obliteration Unit from which he knew his death must come at any moment.

Clustered about the screen in the Governor's office, Sil, the Chief and the Governor, now temporarily revived after the vote-in, watched Jondar's courageous acceptance of his imminent fate.

'This most wonderful entertainment is,' Sil gloated, his tongue flicking in and out like a lizard snaring an insect.

'Sir . . .' Bax entered, his face puzzled and concerned, 'there's a strange unexplained object in the Dome of Punishment.'

'Not now . . .' the Chief said automatically, his eyes never wavering from the video screen where Jondar faced execution.

The troubled Bax tried again: 'But . . .'

'Silence!' Sil screamed 'Can't you see execution is apparent!' Then the Thoros-Betan began to howl with maniacal laughter that quite drowned any further attempt Bax might take to draw attention to the mysterious blue object with *Police Box* written on its side that had appeared on a screen fed by a subsidiary wide-angle camera that was routinely taking a master shot of the imminent Laser Obliteration.

Bax considered speaking out yet again but all his superiors seemed intent only on watching the death of Jondar.

Quietly withdrawing, Bax returned to his screens, determined as far as his duties allowed to continue to monitor the blue rectangular object that had appeared without warning in the execution wing of the Punishment Dome.

In the strange domain Peri had left the TARDIS and followed the Doctor as he stole closer and closer up behind Maldak who seemed intent only on observing the RLBE that now pulsated and filled the chamber with a fierce crimson glow that deepened in intensity as the moment of deadly eruption approached.

When they were within a pace of him, Maldak, to the Doctor's surprise, turned suddenly upon them. Ignoring the energy weapon the guard trained upon him, the Doctor smiled pleasantly and nodded at the shuddering Laser Emitter and the sweating prisoner chained before it. 'Not interrupting anything, are we?'

Maldak blinked then set his expression to one of dour determination.

'I know how this place works. You are but a product of my imagination. I choose – ' At this point Maldak really concentrated. 'I *know* that I must resist you . . . such strange creatures cannot exist except through the Dome exerting its influence on the dark regions of my mind.'

'Quite right,' the Doctor said soothingly.

The young guard stared long and hard at the Doctor and Peri, expecting them to fade like phantoms under the intensity of his gaze.

Confusingly, the Doctor and Peri refused to disappear.

'My . . . my anti-hallucin switch is suffering malfunction.' Maldak's certainty faltered.

'That's right, and we've come to fix it. Right, Peri?'

'Sure.'

'Show me the switch. Come on. At once!' the Doctor snapped authoritatively. Obeying the tone of

24

command, Maldak reached for his helmet, allowing the Doctor to make a grab for the gun.

Locked in a desperate arm-to-arm contest to wrest the weapon from Maldak the pair began to edge towards the shuddering laser grille. Jondar watched Maldak and the Doctor struggle ever nearer, hardly daring to hope for a chance if not to escape at least to be able to strike one blow at his tormentors. Jondar waited and prayed for the hated prison guard to come within reach.

Feeling Maldak's strength of grip on the disputed gun becoming too much for him, the Doctor gambled on a sudden release of his resistance. Staggering away with the weapon, Maldak finally stumbled within range of Jondar's chained wrists. Knowing his opportunity would last only a second, Jondar pounced, smashing down with all his force against the nape of the guard's neck that momentarily was unprotected beneath his helmet.

Groggily, Maldak slumped down onto his knees. Desperately, Jondar struck down again; this time the force of the blow rendered the guard unconscious at his feet.

'Help me!' Jondar roared frantically to the Doctor. 'This laser is due to explode!'

Quickly, the Doctor moved with what seemed to Jondar like agonising calm to the rear of the ominously shuddering Random Laser Beam Emitter and began to examine its technology thoughtfully.

In their home cell Arak was on the edge of his stool with excitement.

'That was a fine bit of action. But he should've jumped on the guard's throat. He'll be coming round in a minute. Look, Etta, he's moving!'

Etta watched the screen as she was required to do.

She couldn't recall such a scenario occurring before but, believing always that the authorities were behind everything and always knew best, she assumed a logical explanation.

'They won't escape,' she said with assurance.

Arak wanted to believe they would. 'Hurry up!' he urged the Doctor who was still fiddling around in the RLBE. 'They'll all blow themselves up in a bit,' Etta smiled smugly and noted the time in her viewstat report.

'Is this planned!' Sil shrilled, then pointed angrily at the Governor's wall screen that showed the Doctor now working furiously to disarm the deadly execution laser beam technology.

'Certainly not.' The Governor frowned then turned to the Chief. 'What's happening in there?' he asked.

Puzzled, the Chief shook his head. 'I'll alert the retrieval squad immediately.'

'Sir!' Bax's panting urgent voice made them all turn from the screen. 'There's another group got into the Punishment Dome.'

'Rebels?' the Governor questioned with distaste and urgency.

'I . . . I don't know.' Bax stammered. 'You all right, sir?' Waves of sickness made the Governor sway on his feet as the after-effects of the cell disintegrator made him stumble for words of reply.

Sil bounced up and down on his water tank in anger at what he took to be shilly-shally and foolish delay.

'Of them all must be apprehended, executed, apprehended!' Sil demanded.

The Governor could not decide what to do.

'Chief . . . you attend to it.' The Governor waved a weary hand and slumped down onto his chair.

'Right away, sir. We will catch them and arrange a

triple execution. Jondar, the intruder and the girl.'

'Splendid!' The alien clapped his tiny green hands and cackled out in crazy glee at the joyful prospect of three deaths rather than one.

4

Escape into Danger

'Ah, yes, of course . . .' The Doctor sighed with some relief as at last he made sense of the intricate Q-switch bypass circuitry. Joining two contact points then simultaneously neutralising their refractive pulse from the photon accelerator, he thus allowed the master switch to become operable and to cut off the build-up of destructive power.

With the RLBE suddenly quiet and still, the jangle of Jondar's chains brought the Doctor's attention back to the condemned man's plight.

'Help me, whoever you are!' Jondar gasped, straining against his steel bonds.

Seeing the taut links gave the Doctor an idea. 'Peri, pull him away from the wall.'

'How?'

'Support him . . . pull the chains tight . . . yes . . . yes . . . that's it . . . good.'

Jondar, supported by Peri, leant away from the wall at an angle, causing the restraining chains to pull into a taut line. Carefully aiming, the Doctor flicked the Q-switch once and a searing bolt flashed across and parted cleanly the chains that had restrained Jondar's left arm.

'Now the other one. Quickly, Peri.'

Jondar swayed across to his left with such alacrity that Peri almost lost her footing. 'Hey, not so fast!'

This time it took four attempts to part the steel chains with a laser bolt but finally the links were cut through causing Jondar to fall free alongside the now rapidly recovering Maldak.

With a growl of hatred Jondar prepared to attack the guard again but the Doctor restrained him; but not before an initial blow had halted Maldak's return to full consciousness.

'No time for that, let's get back to the safety of the TARDIS.'

'What?'

'Over there,' the Doctor started to say, then saw beyond the blue police box a black patrol car swooshing along on a monorail that the Doctor suddenly realised ran down the centre of the gloomy corridor.

'Doctor!'

'Help me. Pull this laser contraption round!'

Peri and Jondar helped the Doctor tug the laser grille around to face the oncoming retrieval squad car and with some readjustment the Doctor set the laser unit to activation again so that beams of force began to stream towards the car which braked and came to a halt under the unexpected laser barrage. However, one foolhardy guard ventured out and died with a scream as a beam scorched through his midriff.

Realising that return to the TARDIS was now impossible the Doctor signalled that they should retreat further into the Punishment Dome. Supporting Jondar, Peri and the Doctor hurried away from the RLBE that was still throwing out its deadly beams towards the stranded car in which the guards were trapped.

Impatiently waiting to resume negotiations with the Governor, Sil was perched on his water tank outside the Governor's office. Scornfully he watched the hurried activity around him as the officers tried to marshall the resources of the Punishment Dome that had been disrupted by the Doctor's sudden arrival. Speaking quietly to one of his black-skinned Thoros-Alphan bearers, Sil allowed his contempt to express itself.

'Seven credits for a unit, when the engineers of every known solar system cry out for Zeiton-7 to power their spacecraft. You, Ber, return to our craft and alert Lord Kiv to have a colonising force standing by in case we have to occupy Varos.'

'Yes, Mentor.' The bearer left his master and hurried away.

Watching him go, Sil contemplated his decision and luxuriated in its possible consequences. 'If I control this planet and its mineral resources I will possess the means of power throughout this whole galaxy and perhaps all others beyond.' The thought was so seductive, the vision of power so overwhelming, that Sil bounced up and down with utter pleasure. It was an uncontrolled movement that made him lose balance and fall with a splash! into the murky interior of his tank. Sil's good humour disappeared; spitting out fluid he surfaced to discover a still wearied Governor staring down at him.

'This is no time for a swim, Sil.'

'Wha . . . I . . . you!' Sil spluttered for once lost for words.

'Can we resume sensible negotiations?' the Governor asked curtly and returned to his office, leaving an irate alien to gather the shreds of his dignity as best he could.

The Chief Officer, when he saw the Doctor halt the advance of the retrieval car, was the first to act by ordering PD control to sever the power connection of the Laser Beam Emitter so as to allow the guards to go forward in urgent pursuit of the intruders.

Arak avidly watched the camera shots on his wall screen which cut between the area of the Dome that contained the Doctor, Jondar and Peri and the speeding mobile patrol car.

Weakened by his long ordeal, Jondar began to fall behind the Doctor and Peri. The Doctor turned to the exhausted young man and tried to encourage him on.

'You said there might be a way of escape this way?'

'Yes . . . I thought . . .'

Peri, having explored the corridor a little further along, returned with grim news.

'It's a dead end, Doctor.'

'Yes, all right.' The Doctor hardly acknowledged his companion; all his attention now seemed to be focused on the glowing red eye of a camera placed up above them and even now beaming their worried stares back onto every home screen of Varos.

'What is this place?' the Doctor asked Jondar quietly.

'An ordinary prison once . . .' the rebel broke off, listening to a low buzzing sound in an adjoining passage.

'There's a patrol car coming!'

'Let's try and halt their progress then.' The Doctor stepped decisively across and pulled the camera cable from the wall, beckoned Jondar urgently to him and, after threading the remains of a wrist chain between the cable and the wall, urged the rebel to heave with all his might. After several tugs the cable eventually pulled away from its wall clamps under their joint pressure, bringing the camera crashing down with a shower of glowing sparks as the circuits shorted furiously under the impact of the fall.

Seizing the cable, the Doctor guided the sparking camera towards the monorail. When both power sources touched there was a blinding flash that instantly plunged the corridor into darkness. In the moment's silence that followed nothing could be heard of the patrol car in the next corridor. For the moment the

31

Doctor had succeeded in halting the pursuit – but for how long? Trapped in a dead end, there seemed little gain and already the trio could hear the thudding boots of the guards charging nearer and nearer; the flash of a beam of light on the wall at the end of the passage meant for sure that at any moment their presence would be revealed and their capture completed.

Backing away from the bobbing light that any second would find them, the Doctor felt a cool touch on the skin of his neck. Turning, he heard a woman's voice speaking low and urgently into his ear.

'This way . . . through here . . .'

'Well, if you insist,' the Doctor replied, and stepped through an open concealed wall panel into an old disused cell. Peri was followed by Jondar who, on seeing their rescuer, cried out in delighted surprise.

'Areta!'

Holding her fingers to his lips, Areta, a lithe, blonde girl in her late teens slid the wall panel back into place, covered her flashlight, and waited tensely while the guards prowled past outside.

Through cracks in the wall they could all see the guards' torchlight spill through with occasional glimmers of light. But then, thankfully, there was darkness and quiet before the lights came on again as power was restored throughout the Punishment Dome.

Embracing, Areta and Jondar stared in wonderment at each other.

Areta began first: 'I thought we'd lost you . . . they set up your execution so quickly we couldn't stage even an attempt at a rescue.'

Jondar frowned, nodded towards the Doctor and Peri. 'I thought he was sent by you.'

'No.'

'I will explain,' the Doctor said, 'but I'd sooner return to my TARDIS.'

The young couple glanced at each other.

32

'TAR – ?' Jondar began, not understanding.

'Ship.'

'Spaceship?'

'Something like that. Ah!' Peri was interrupted by the frightening intrusion of a uniformed guard into the cell through the secret wall panel.

The Doctor also reacted with apprehension but a smiling Areta immediately calmed their fears.

'It's all right. Rondel has agreed to help us escape through the guards' entrance.'

'We mustn't delay. I must report for guard duty soon.' The guard seemed friendly though obviously uneasy at the risk he was taking.

'What is this place?' the Doctor asked.

Jondar's voice became bitter. 'Where the innocent suffer while the population gloats over our sufferings.'

'Not all of us,' the guard protested.

'No. Not you, Rondel.' Areta smiled at the guard and put a comforting arm about the agitated Jondar who addressed the Doctor and Peri. 'Varos was a prison planet once, a colony for the criminal and insane. The descendants of the original officers still rule. The rest of us toil and exist without hope.'

The Doctor could hardly believe what he was hearing. 'But you have precious mineral deposits – Zeiton-7.'

An expression of disinterest appeared on Jondar's face. 'That stuff. Who wants it?'

'I wouldn't say no to a little,' the Doctor said thoughtfully.

'We must go,' Rondel insisted, then began cautiously to slide aside the wall panel that would allow them to return to the main part of the Dome.

Looking warily out, Rondel signalled back that all seemed quiet, the patrol guards having apparently moved on to search another sector.

Following the guard out into the corridor, the Doctor

was the first to see the uniform patrol leader step menacingly around the corner of the passageway.

'Look out!' the Doctor yelled as the *phud!* of the energy weapon sounded and Rondel simultaneously choked, staggered and fell forward, the flesh of his throat torn open by the impact of the energised missile shot from the weapon held by the advancing patrol leader.

The Doctor could hear the sound of other running feet. With Rondel obviously dead there seemed nowhere to go but back into the cell. Once inside the Doctor closed the wall panel and stared at the dismayed trio before him. 'Any ideas before they break down the wall and we are obliterated?' he asked calmly.

5

The Purple Zone

'There's another exit, but away from the main prison section.'

'Where does it lead?' Peri started to ask but was interrupted by the Doctor.

'No time for that, Peri,' he said impatiently. 'Let's go.'

Areta pulled aside a grey stained canvas curtain that had merged almost to invisibility against the dull stone walls of the dusty cell. Behind the curtain a dark hole gaped where blocks of stone had been removed. Beyond that nothing could be seen but Stygian darkness. As she scrambled through the gap Peri could smell the musty air of disuse and decay that seemed appropriate, given the dead dreams and ruined hopes that must have perished within the labyrinth of despair in which they now found themselves adrift.

Stumbling, clinging each to the other, they made their way blindly forward with Areta leading them to what she prayed would be a way back into the main section of the Punishment Dome. Travelling in the darkness, they would sometimes pass a more populated area of the prison. At first Peri thought she must be near a sea but then she realised that what she could hear was the rise and fall of the misery of the prisoners' groans and cries for mercy from what horrors Peri dared not imagine as she groped blindly forward after the others in the sealed and forgotten catacombs.

Just as it seemed they must wander the rat-infested corridors of the old prison endlessly Jondar noticed a bright crack of light running down a walled-off passageway up ahead.

Areta saw it too and sighed with relief.

'Rondel mentioned another secret way into the Dome. This must be it.'

'Into, not out of?' the Doctor queried.

'Yes. The only exits are controlled by the Dome guards except for these secret inner access doors, constructed by prisoners over the years.'

Jondar began to search for the location of the false stone that would cause the wall to open and to allow them into the next sector of the Dome. Seven stones down, the slab tilted and the wall opened into a dimly-lit passageway that was empty except for a camera that glowed as it detected their presence.

Noticing this, the Doctor asked, 'The cameras . . . they feed pictures from here into every home?'

'And into the guard control points. The whole Dome is wired,' Jondar explained as they closed the panel and moved away out of the range of the spying camera. The Doctor noted that Areta's alert and fearful gaze darted hither and thither as if she expected danger everywhere. Noticing the Doctor's glance, Areta waved a tense hand around at the seemingly featureless rock of the corridor. 'Areas of danger lurk around every corner . . . you can die in oh so many ingenious ways.'

'Areta's right,' Jondar added grimly. 'But the cruellest thing is that there is supposed to be a safe route leading towards the exit. Anyone who finds that way out must automatically be granted pardon and freedom.'

The Doctor brightened. 'So there's hope?'

Jondar and Areta exchanged glances that reflected a weary cynicism. 'It's another trick of the officers . . .'

'You're certain?'

'No. But everything else is.'

'Ah. Well, we'd better get back to my TARDIS; that way we can all escape instantly.'

'How?' Jondar frowned, not understanding.

'You find our way back there and the Doc will be only too pleased to demonstrate,' said Peri and then shivered as a chill draught of air passed over them as they reached a junction of the passageways. Jondar looked cautiously first one way then the other, Areta's eyes never leaving his face as if she still needed to convince herself that her man had indeed succeeded in cheating death. But how long, she wondered.

'Do you know where we are, Jondar?' she asked quietly.

'Oh, yes. Near the Purple Zone adjoining the execution area.'

Areta's expression became woebegone.

'Purple Zone?' the Doctor started to ask.

'If we are to get back to your ship, the only way I know is through that sector,' replied Jondar, grimly.

'Then we're as good as dead,' Areta muttered.

'Rubbish!' the Doctor said abruptly and immediately strode along the corridor away from the others. Startled, Jondar turned to Peri.

'Is he sane, this Doctor?'

'Sometimes.'

'But this obviously isn't one of those times?'

'Peri!' the Doctor called back. 'This is no time for casual conversation.'

'Coming!' More out of habit than sense, Peri hurried after the Doctor. Shaking their heads, Jondar and Areta reluctantly began to follow in the wake of what they believed must be a foolhardy madman who was leading them all towards certain destruction within the notorious Purple Zone.

They had almost caught up with the Doctor when suddenly all about them the walls, ceiling, floor, the

37

atmosphere itself began to assume a tinge of crimson, then violet, then a merging that became a deep purple which completely enclosed their vision.

'Pretty . . . pretty . . .' said the Doctor admiringly. 'It does improve the look of the place, don't you think?'

The others didn't reply but blinked and stared about them fearfully as their optic nerves tried to adjust to the eerie change of light that now washed over their strained features.

Arak chortled as he stared at the purple figures on his wall screen.

'I like this section, Etta. I wonder if the rebos know what's waitin'?'

'They'll soon find out.' Etta bent over her report sheet and drew a neat line ready for the conclusion of a fatal incident report.

Within the haze of purple the air seemed heavy and the Doctor could hear his companions behind him breathing in short painful gulps, whether through fear of the unknown or through a genuine lack of oxygen he couldn't decide.

Peri was the first to hear the angry buzz behind them. Fearfully, she looked back and screamed in terror at the huge black yellow-eyed demon that was bearing down upon them at frightening speed.

'Get down!' the Doctor shouted, his two hearts thumping wildly on either side of his chest. The frenzied creature zoomed over them, its wings vibrating with such force that they felt flattened by its passing.

Their demon attacker turned and hovered malevolently, preparing for attack. The Doctor stared at the massive black body covered in a fur that banded into green circular stripes and the six black legs dangling and glistening in the purple light. The thing grated frenetically, its wings jarring as it began to hurtle towards them.

Mesmerised, the Doctor found himself staring into the many-faceted yellow eyes that grew bigger by the microsecond as the monster bore down upon them. In the fragment of time left to him the Doctor's mind noted the probing antennae and the grotesque sucking tube dangling from what must be a mouth. Take away the massive size of the inverberate and it would be nothing more than . . . With a jolt the Doctor realised what it was that was hurtling down upon them, hell-bent on their destruction.

'Close your eyes!' he yelled, hoping that the others would follow. He clamped his eyelids closed knowing that his theory would be instantly verified either by safety or oblivion.

With their eyes closed, the roaring, gyrating sound of their attacker immediately disappeared. The whirring of the wings ceased and the blast they had caused was felt no more.

'Don't open your eyes yet, make yourselves blind until I say look!' the Doctor reached behind him. 'My hand, Peri, try and find it . . . yes, there . . . good; Jondar, Areta . . . over here . . . eyes tightly closed . . . keep trying to link . . . but don't whatever you do look about you.'

After much blind fumbling the four finally linked up and, clambering awkwardly to their feet, stumbled along instinctively, led by the Doctor who insisted that their eyes should not open until he gave the word that it was safe to do so. After much bumping into walls and each other, the Doctor called a halt and ventured a peep through barely open eyelids. They seemed about a dozen paces from the end of the Purple Zone but behind them the Doctor became aware again that an angry, grinding, ominous note was sounding. That meant the beginning of another attack. Closing his eyes, the Doctor dashed forward, pulling his party with him.

After counting thirteen paces and adding one for luck the Doctor risked another peek and discovered to his relief that the Purple Zone had disappeared; once more they were in a seemingly unremarkable grey stone passage, similar to many others that honeycombed the Punishment Dome.

Staring at the three others who still stood, eyes closed, holding hands the Doctor smiled.

'It's OK. You can wake up now.' Cautiously the trio peered about them and saw only the empty corridor.

'Wha . . ?' Jondar began.

'The Purple . . .' Areta said.

'What's happened?' Peri demanded.

Hearing a slight buzz nearby, the Doctor made a quick grab and closed his hand. After plucking a tiny object from the air and cupping one hand over the other, he grinned at his companions.

'Let me show you your monstrous attacker . . . the fearsome flying monster of Varos . . .'

Opening his hands he invited inspection of the tiny buzzing object held in captivity by the palms of his hands.

'A gee-jee fly.' Startled, Areta glanced at Jondar for confirmation.

'Yes. A common harmless little fly,' said the Doctor.

Peri stared at the tiny insect. 'But the thing that attacked us just now was fearsome, a creature from my worst imaginings.'

Areta agreed, 'It was huge . . .'

'No, we only thought it was,' the Doctor explained. 'I don't quite understand how, but what we saw was a distortion of our perceptions. This little fly was some-how distorted by the purple light so that our faculty of sight told our brain that this little chap was a huge predatory insect and not a harmless little fly.' the Doctor paused, opened his hands and watched the tiny gee-jee fly away. 'When we got through the Purple Zone when we eliminated that light by closing our eyes we returned to a sense of proper proportions. Interesting . . .'

The Doctor began to muse, to look about him at the walls, the ceiling, and at the ever-present cameras which watched them unceasingly. The Doctor waved a casual greeting to whoever might be watching, hardly realising that meant most of the population of Varos huddled in their spartan home-cells protected by the Domes that littered the harsh surface of Varos.

In the main communications centre Bax continued to monitor the Punishment Dome with particular interest. The Doctor and his companions had lasted much longer than the usual run of miscreants and already the centre was receiving many expressions of appreciation and requests for information as to their identity.

Sil and the Chief discussing the still abortive negotiations over the price of Zeiton ore entered Bax's work station just in time to witness the Doctor's cheery wave at the camera in the Punishment Zone.

'They still alive!' Sil squealed in anger at the sight of the Doctor's defiance.

The Chief didn't share Sil's reaction. He had noted the rebel party entering the Purple Zone and had assumed the usual antics of fear that caused comic mental disorientation leading to heart failure and apoplexy. But here was the strange fair-haired intruder and his party who had evidently traversed the ordeal, apparently without undue concern.

'He's not a fool, the man in the patchwork coat,' the Chief said, gruffly.

Bax nodded. 'Or maybe he's just lucky.'

The Chief stared at the screen thoughtfully. 'Or they have received information on how the Dome works. There was a guard killed who was helping them.'

Shaking his head, Bax turned to the Chief and Sil. 'The Prison contains many devices; no one could know or survive them all.'

Sil glared at the monitor screen that showed the Doctor now examining the walls carefully. 'They do not act or seem like Varosians . . .' Then an awful thought penetrated the crafty mind of the little Thoros-Betan. 'They could be from a rival company, the Amorb Prospecting Division.' Sil trembled with fear and rage at the prospect of business competitors discovering that the long term contract for Zeiton Ore was still unsigned and open for bids that would escalate the asking price.

'Remove them immediately!' he demanded of the Chief.

'Why? They are providing excellent entertainment.'

'If they are from Amorb I want them questioned and killed before this Governor gets wind of the possibility of rival bidders!'

The Chief understood the dangers in that possibility not only for Sil but for his own huge income from secret pay-offs by the Mentors of Thoros-Beta.

'Get me a line to internal prison control!' he snapped at Bax.

'Yes, Chief.' The technician obeyed dutifully, wondering why there was need for such urgency.

'After that, Bax, inform them that the object found near the execution site must be brought in for inspection.'

'And quickly, quickly!' spluttered Sil, swaying dangerously on the rim of his water tank.

The Chief put out a restraining hand to steady the little green alien.

42

'Don't worry, my dear Sil, we'll have them in and under interrogation soon.'

'Do that you'd better,' Sil's voice box rattled out. 'Or I will request that you be given to your colleague – what is his name?' One of his bearers bent to Sil and whispered. Sil smirked up at the burly Chief. 'Quillam.'

'Oh, him . . .' The Chief pretended an indifference that he was far from feeling. How had Sil found out about the arch-interrogator and deviser of the delights of the Punishment Dome who usually stayed underground, despising the officers and prisoners alike? What was going on? The Chief could not decide any more. There were suddenly too many dangers in the situation. Some had to be removed: starting with the rebels and the mysterious stranger who appeared to be leading them. Death. Yes. No fancy devices, just clean, quick, final. Then there would be no need to involve the likes of the loathsome Mr Quillam and his fanatical minions.

'I'll attend to their capture personally,' the Chief said and strode away purposefully.

'You had better!' Sil shrieked then began to cackle hysterically, his own fear of failure giving an edge of mania to the already freakish sound.

6

Capture!

'Doctor, we can't stay here.'

'No, you're right. I was looking for a circuit trigger but if it exists it must be well hidden . . .' The Doctor straightened from his survey of the rocky walls. 'Perception distorters must have something to activate them so that we can imagine the horrors they might contain. But I can't see anything . . . strange.'

Peri looked up and down the empty corridor and heard a distant rumbling sound.

'Is everything we experience here imaginary?'

'No,' answered Jondar as they began to move away from the now quiescent Purple Zone. 'Some dangers are very real. The crowd loves to watch trialists face a danger that they think must be imaginary.'

The Doctor nodded. 'But one the viewers know is real.'

'Yes,' Areta cut in. 'They love to shout and applaud as fools like us walk towards certain death.'

Peri was horrified by what she was hearing. '*Who* loves to watch such things?'

'Almost everyone on Varos,' Jondar replied. 'It's the way the officers divert discontent, questions, thoughts of revolution.'

'But not everyone, not you.'

Jondar and Areta looked at each other with a hopeless tenderness that Peri found touching. The young man shrugged fatalistically. 'What good does our defiance

44

do? We will perish here, our deaths providing only a moment's entertainment.'

The Doctor thrust his chin forward pugnaciously. Peri recognised the signs: she had seen that determination many times before. A demonstration of spirit that said no matter what odds or forces ranged against us we will oppose with strength, ingenuity and cunning if need be. Areta and Jondar stared in quiet disbelief as the Doctor spoke firmly to them.

'We will not succumb quietly. If we perish here it will not be because of our own belief that we cannot win through. If there's an exit out of this fun palace I suggest we make every effort to find it. Starting now.' And with that the Doctor turned on his heel and began to walk briskly down the darkened corridor.

'Which way are they going?' Arak asked Etta excitedly.

'Left,' came the laconic reply.

Arak concentrated on trying to remember what other trialists had encountered in the direction now taken by the Doctor's party. 'What's that way then?'

'Like those rebos you'll just have to wait and see what's coming, won't you, Arak?'

'Right, I will,' he muttered, peering at his wall screen and distinguishing the glaring eyes of some giant beast that was obviously lying in wait for the Doctor and his companions who were about to turn a corner and set foot into its lair.

Through the ambionic sound system speakers that were placed in each corner of their cell a throbbing low reverberating roar began to be heard. At first it sounded like far thunder then like an advancing rumbling tidal wave of sound. The guttural coughing roar chilled the viewers of Varos. They shivered in terror and stared at the four victims transfixed by the sound and fury of the beast whose wrath was about to fall upon them.

Peri stared into the luminescent green eyes and felt the volition drain from her limbs. The deep coughing sound thundered out again, bouncing and magnifying as the sound waves reflected from the rocks about them. Then came the stench of carrion beneath.

'Ugh!' Next to Peri, Areta, turned her head and covered her face with cupped hands in a vain attempt to escape the sight and smell of the loathsome predator which crouched in the darkness before them.

'Run, Doctor!' Jondar urged.

'Is it animal?' the Doctor enquired in a matter-of-fact way, standing his ground.

'Smells like it.'

'Or is that just illusion?'

Jondar considered. 'Just be like Comm Div Design to site a real live monster immediately after a distort section like the Purple Zone.'

'Yes,' the Doctor agreed. 'Or is that exactly how a master planner would expect us to reason?'

The Doctor's speculation did little to comfort the others and he saw their fear become deeper as the great eyes glowered upon them and the bellowing roar began to threaten again.

'Oh, well. I suppose one of us had better find out if this fellow's as fierce as he pretends to be.'

Jondar tried to prevent the Doctor's suicidal dash towards the glittering opal eyes but he was a microsecond too late. Peri cried out after her companion but the Doctor had disappeared into the darkness. Tensely, the three remaining listened to hear the bone-crunching snap of teeth masticating on a tasty morsel.

Then a cheery voice called out to them and announced, 'Come on, it's quite harmless . . . just a couple of lights, a fan for nasty smells and a box of sound effects.'

Sheepishly Peri, Areta and Jondar traipsed along to

join the Doctor who was standing grinning amongst a couple of green arc lights rigged on either side of the passageway. The Doctor pointed to a small iron grating let into the wall. 'An air pump sending out the "sweet aroma". How do these things activate? Something must trigger all these delights.'

'Never mind that, Doctor.' Peri frowned at the Doctor's insatiable curiosity.

Jondar was glancing about thoughtfully. 'I'm sure we are near to where I was almost laserised.'

'That's near the TARDIS.' Peri nudged the Doctor hard and, as he still seemed lost in thought, she decided to do it again with increased force.

'*Ow!*'

'Doc, I've seen enough of this dump. Let's go!'

'All right.' The Doctor allowed himself to be shepherded along to where the TARDIS had materialised, as it seemed to Peri, days before but was, she realised, only a few crowded hours ago.

Satisfied that order was about to be restored in the Dome, the Chief had returned to the Communications Centre to find a worried Bax punching up appreciation figures on a computer screen. 'The viewpop like them, Chief. We've received Dome-high appreciation figures.'

Far from appearing bothered at the Doctor's growing popularity, the Chief rubbed his hands in anticipation. 'Good, good. All the more impact when they are captured, tried and executed. A rebel leader, his woman, and intruders from another world. Not only will their dispatch fill prime time on Varos but the recording of their final agonies should sell a million copies throughout the civilised worlds.'

Bax could see nothing incongruous in the Chief's statement. To Varosians such cruelties were but a part of everyday life: something to witness, and enjoy all the more because the mere fact that you could witness someone else's suffering meant that at least there was somebody more unfortunate than yourself.

'Where are they now?' The Chief peered at the main screen.

'Almost where they first appeared.'

'Ah, good.' The Chief chuckled. Wondering what had restored his superior's humour, Bax concentrated on his task and brought the Doctor into close-up to reveal an expressive look of surprise and consternation.

'The TARDIS . . .' the Doctor began.

'Gone,' groaned Peri hopelessly.

'It was just here,' the Doctor muttered, checking his bearing and seeing the RLBE grille leaning askew down an adjacent corridor.

'Your ship has gone?'

'Yes, Areta. 'Fraid so.'

'We must find it!'

'Not to panic, Peri, please. It must be around somewhere . . . Come on, come on . . . it has to be found.'

'Doctor!' Peri protested not wishing to experience any more of the Punishment Dome's nasty surprises but it was too late. The Doctor was on his way into another area of the frightening warren of ordeal into which they had blundered.

Along with the Governor, Sil shook his head in bewilderment at the Doctor's continued survival. 'This mysterious most is . . .'

'There has to be an explanation for their presence. The strangers will be captured soon, then we'll force some answers. Right, Chief?' The Governor turned to the Chief who had just joined them in the office.

'Yes, of course.'

Sil was not satisfied by the officer's apparent confidence. 'I would wish them dead. Only that would please my company for keeps.'

The Governor could not quite understand why the little alien was angrier and even more insistent on getting his way than usual. However, the Governor sensed, Sil did seem more willing to move from his intransigent bargaining position; perhaps it might be as well to placate him further.

'Close them out, Chief. Use every guard available. I will make a broadcast to the viewers of Varos and explain what is occurring on their screens and why.'

The Chief saluted. 'We have also captured their spaceship. At this moment our engineers are attempting to blast their way inside.'

'Good, carry on.'

'Sir.' The Chief glanced at Sil, but the green angry features gave nothing back in support or approval. If there was a glint in those deep-set yellow eyes it could only be one of warning the Chief to succeed or accept the consequences of Sil revealing his treachery over concealing the true worth of the Zeiton-7 ore from the Governor and his people. Deciding to redouble his efforts to eliminate the rebels, the Chief, goaded into action by fear and greed, hurried away from the Governor's office.

Expecting trouble around every corner, Peri was staying close to the Doctor but surprisingly, for once, nothing untoward seemed to be happening within the Dome, though very shortly they were to discover why the Dome had become inactive.

'Guards!' yelled Jondar suddenly from behind them.

One darting glance by the others confirmed Jondar's shout of warning. A black snub-nosed patrol car, full of

49

armed guards, was powering towards them. Flashes of force bolt emission could be seen simultaneously with a scorching passage of laser shafts shooting above them.

There was no need to tell everyone to run. The panic and fear made the fugitives hit their stride as one. Hearts pounding, legs pumping, all four just made the next corner safely.

Confusingly they found themselves facing a junction of passageways and, with but an instant to decide direction, the Doctor chose the right while the others at the same instant took the fork to the left.

Turning the corner a moment later the patrol car veered left and soon closed upon the three fleeing rebels. After giving a warning yell that failure to stop would mean obliteration the car commander sent a warning laser blast above the heads of Jondar and smiled with cruel satisfaction as the two women slowed and halted. A moment later the man halted his escape bid and dejectedly joined them in surrender.

'Inside the car!' The commander motioned with his laser weapon. There was nothing else to do; with a last resigned look of despair down the empty corridor Peri ducked inside the patrol car where her wrists were handcuffed then chained to a steel restraining bar. There she huddled next to Areta and Jondar who were already pinioned. By this uncomfortable means they were taken into captivity there to await their final starring roles in future 'entertainments' that would be mounted within the domain whose existence depended on the taking of innocent lives for vengeance and profit.

7

Death in the Desert

When the patrol car reached the heavily-guarded exit
from the Dome, Peri, Areta and Jondar were released
from their chains and forced to step out into a harshly lit
white-tiled area. Peri blinked under the fierce light of
the prison reception centre. A shadow before her
allowed the girl's sight to focus. The young guard she
and the Doctor had first encountered when leaving the
TARDIS was standing before her, his mouth hard and
set.

'Make a fool of me would you!' he spat out venomously as the back of his hand snapped across Peri's face.

Shocked and hurt, Peri fell to the ground. On her
knees and expecting further reprisals, she was relieved
when the commander restrained Maldak. 'Do not
damage her – she is to be taken to the Communications
Centre while these two are to be returned to the Termi-
nation Cell.'

'Sir!' Maldak saluted and then pulled Peri roughly to
her feet.

'Communication Centre?' Peri stammered.

'Shut up!' Maldak pushed her ahead of him towards
the waiting patrol car.

Deep inside the Punishment Dome the Doctor paused,
lungs straining, from his race to escape capture.
Listening for sounds of pursuit, he then crouched down

51

to try and detect any vibration from the steel power line that ran down the centre of the corridor floor. The Doctor could hear no sound or movement. Still out of breath, he gained control of his heaving lungs then realised how uncomfortably close and sticky the atmosphere had become. Perspiring, he loosened his collar and began to trudge on into the area ahead that seemed a little better illuminated than the section he had just left behind.

Another half a dozen steps and the light was distinctly brighter and the temperature far warmer. The Doctor suddenly realised what was happening and with a rapid turnabout he charged back the way he had just come only to cannon into a steel mesh grille that had silently dropped down and now barred any possibility of retreat. Rattling the mesh only revealed to the Doctor how strong the grille was. There was only one real choice to make if he was not to remain trapped against the steel barrier and that was to venture onwards.

The Doctor's steel blue eyes peered into the blaze of light ahead of him and with some trepidation he began cautiously to move towards its radiance.

Etta and Arak stared at their wall screen with differing emotions as they watched the Doctor becoming bathed in an increasing intensity of light.

'He won't survive this time,' Etta spoke softly with perhaps a tinge of regret as if, despite herself, she was beginning to become involved with the Doctor's prolonged battle for survival.

Abruptly the picture on the video screen changed to the logo of the flashing Varos initial that always preceded a government announcement.

Arak groaned theatrically, partly at the disruption of the camera pictures that showed the Doctor's progress and partly because of his boredom with the seemingly endless succession of governmental announcements and vote-ins.

After the 'V' logo faded, the smiling face of the Governor appeared in mid close-up on their screen.

'Oh, no, what's he want?' Arak moaned petulantly.

'Shut up and listen!' his wife snapped as the Governor began to address the viewers of Varos.

'I must report that the attempt to divert the course of justice has been repelled. The rebel Jondar and his compatriots have either been captured or destroyed. The extent of the rebellion is, however, far greater than first imagined and aid from another source – perhaps from another world – is suspected.' The Governor paused to allow the implication to sink into the viewers' minds then continued with practised measured warmth.

'The warship of their invasion has now been captured by my officer guard. The leader of the aggressors, as you have just seen, is, at this very moment, walking into a no-options kill centre; there he will suffer the fate of all who seek to overturn the law of Varos!'

The Governor sighed gently as if what was about to occur next was nothing but a formality. 'There is, of course, as that law requires, the need for a vote of approval or' – this with a faint smile – 'disapproval. I await your verdict.' The Governor leant back in his chair, waiting for the vote that would either devastate his metabolism or pour down beneficence that would invigorate his being and bring renewed energy for the difficult task of ruling Varos.

The light of the sun was blinding the Doctor. His throat felt parched and cracked like the bed of a long dried-up river. He stared into the distance, seeing only mile upon distant mile of red desert landscape stretching ahead. The burning surface of the sand below the soles of his shoes began to send fiery rays through to his feet with the promise of increasing torment to come as each step followed the next. Glancing behind, the Doctor could see the imprints of his footsteps on the red grit leading from wherever it was he had come from.

Frowning he realised that he could not remember where exactly that was. Confusedly he shook his wild mop of ash-blonde curls from side to side trying to clear his brain and restore clarity to his memory. Nothing changed. The desert environment, harsh and arid, remained unforgiving in its burning intensity.

The vote in the home cell of Arak and Etta was as usual divided for and against, but this was not typical of the voters' response in general for the population did much as the Governor had shrewdly guessed they would. Promised the possibility of watching novel executions on TV, most viewers voted for the Governor's measures without pausing to consider that all they had been given as evidence of insurrection was the doubtful word of their rulers. Even so the Governor strapped in his chair waited tensely, watching the vote totals mount for and against. When a margin of seven to one in his favour became clearly apparent he allowed himself the luxury of relaxation as from above began the sparkling cascade of invigoration that almost restored the cellular damage that had occurred earlier when he had suffered painful defeat at the polls.

When the first stirrings of the simoon wind breathed across the Doctor's broad forehead he was grateful for their relief but the zephyr soon became a stiff breeze that grew rapidly into a driving tormenting force which whipped stinging sand into his now reddened and streaming eyes. The lashing wind then lowered abruptly into a monotonous keening presence that tormented by its very constancy. Wearily, the Doctor made himself trudge on until he could hardly summon the strength to push one throbbing foot past the other.

'Back . . . must . . . go . . . back . . .' he muttered to himself, halting, tired out and sand-blown, swaying under the maddening constantly prying wind. Squinting, then turning, the Doctor searched for his footprints that would lead him back to wherever it was he had journeyed from. Seeing nothing he realised, with a lurch of panic, that the simoon wind had swept away all trace of his steps. All around was sand. Desert. Arid miles of searing red grit that reflected heat under a flaring sun that pulsated with a stream of rays that shrivelled everything that it encountered below.

Just as suddenly as it had attacked the Doctor the force of the wind slackened and dropped to a whisper that stirred the sand against his shoes and now seemed as nothing after the blast of torment it had achieved before. Thirsty and dehydrated from his exertions the Doctor peered ahead into what appeared to be a dreamy haze. He brushed the air before his eyes to clear his vision but still the heat distortion shimmered ahead. Then, magically, the burnished landscape faded and a verdant green island of palm trees with a cool flowing stream appeared, on the far bank of which a peacock strutted accompanied by a familiar figure.

'What?' the Doctor croaked confusedly and stumbled forward as he realised that the figure in blue blouse and shorts was waving, beckoning with one arm while holding in her other hand a silver salver that supported a gleaming ice bucket and a tall green pear-shaped bottle of sparkling mineral water.

'Peri!' the Doctor shouted hoarsely, stumbling and forcing himself through the clinging sand that grew ever more resistant with each frantic clumsy stride. The Doctor made towards the oasis and the cool blue figure of Peri and the longed-for refreshment of iced water which she held so invitingly towards him.

'Peri . . . Peri!' the Doctor forced out through his cracked lips as, cruelly, the vision receded, leaving only a shimmer of empty air as the Doctor once more found himself utterly alone in the harsh desert landscape.

Mockingly, the cruel simoon wind began to rise once more and whipped up the particles of hot sand against skin still raw and ravaged from its previous onslaught. The sand was everywhere, under eyelids, in eyes, ears, mouth; choking, spitting, the Doctor tried to clear his dry, dust-filled throat but the wind forced yet more scorching sand upon him until, heaving for breath, he fell to his knees. There seemed no escape except oblivion. The Doctor coughed, fell forward prostate on the ground, hauled himself up onto his elbows then rolled onto his back and stared upwards into the merciless molten glaring eye of the sun. Then his body separated from his spirit and moved no more.

'Gur . . . gur . . . gur-gaargh!' The sound of Sil's maniacal laughter filled the communication centre where Sil, the Chief, Governor and Bax had been watching the Doctor's struggle for existence in an empty corridor of the Punishment Dome that contained not one grain of sand.

Over Sil's continuing cackle of laughter the Chief shook his head wonderingly. 'What a wonderful thing a mind is. The hallucinatory inductor makes him believe he cannot survive and soon he cannot even draw one breath after the next.'

'It was a very fine joke,' Sil gasped. 'Thank you for such fine entertainment, Governor.'

'My pleasure,' the Governor replied formally but felt

a vague dissatisfaction which he found hard to understand; after all, the death of the Doctor was only the latest of so many others he had witnessed.

Arak, staring at his screen that still showed the inert body of the Doctor, licked his lips. 'We got anything to drink, Etta?' he asked, suddenly feeling a deep thirst as if he too had been battling against a sandstorm driven by a simoon wind.

'Go and look,' his wife said, staring unblinkingly at the screen before her.

'What now, sir?' Bax turned to the Governor.

'Go in close, establish there is no flicker of life.'

'Yes, sir.' Bax shifted his cameras into a big close-up that brought the Doctor's waxen face so close that it filled the screen. Not a muscle twitched nor was a tremor of breath evident.

'He's dead, sir.'

'I agree.' The Governor watched the Doctor for a moment more than snapped his fingers.

'Cut it now, Bax,' he ordered and watched the technician terminate the transmission by a flick of a switch that brought up the station 'V' logo and the mournful military march that always played as the evening's entertainment from the Punishment Dome drew to a close.

8

Night and Silence

The Governor lay back in his official transport car and watched the harsh landscape of Varos pass outside the clear plastic tubing that surrounded the monorail that propelled the car. Various lighted domes of differing sizes loomed and passed like giant globules of light scattered about the pitted rocky surface.

As the monorail curved into the docking bay and glided to a halt the Governor felt so tired from the mental and physical battering of the day that he felt hardly able to haul himself out of the padded leather seating and go into the special luxury dome reserved for himself and the rest of the officer guard.

Dragging himself along, he entered the transition bay, pressed the entry button and watched the numbers flash by as the underfloor traction belt carried him smoothly towards his spacious living quarters. His trusty, Sevrin, was waiting to help the Governor through the doorway whose panels had opened noiselessly on recognising the particular aura of the leader's body.

'Bath, sir?' The ageing servant unbuckled the black leather belt and reverently lifted the sash of office from the grey serge uniform of the Governor before placing it carefully in the special wardrobe kept for the trappings of state while the Governor wandered towards the splashing sounds of a bath filling.

The bathroom was large and marbled with twin gold

cherubim that held water flagons that poured precious water into a deep oval sunken bath. Yellow and black Polva plants and imported black orchids filled the corners of the mirrored opulent room. Sighing with pleasure the Governor slipped into the warm welcoming water and luxuriated in its comforting and refreshing depths.

'Sir . . .' Sevrin lowered a tray to him with a bottle of wine and glasses.

'Thank you.' The drink, blue and sparkling, was the Governor's favourite vintage from the vineyards of the planet Emsidium. The first sip brought a sharp invigorating tang on his palate which was followed by the mellow flush of well-being as the famous wine achieved its familiar conquest of fear and depression. Idly the Governor waggled a foot, watching the water cascade from ankle and calf. Born to the officer class he had no troubling thoughts as to why he should not enjoy comfort and wealth while the rest of the population of Varos suffered poverty and deprivation. It had always been like this for the chosen few officer families who ruled the former prison planet. How sweet their life was remained a secret kept from the rest of Varos.

Maybe it was right, thought the Governor, that those unfortunate enough to be chosen by the hazard stakes should enjoy the sweet fruits of life while they could. The Governor remembered how the lots had been cast, how the white box with eleven black squares and one red had been shaken before all his brother officers had plunged their right hands in and grasped a square, holding their choice concealed until the Chief Officer had commanded a show. The officers as one thrust out arms and opened the palms of hands like a black-centred flower with one rogue square of crimson held by the officer whose fate was to become the forty-fifth Governor of Varos. Troubled by the memory, his body stirred in the water, made uneasy by the thoughts of his election to the Governor's chair.

59

'There is no better way,' the Governor muttered to himself and immersed his blonde head beneath the surface of the water and blew slow bubbles of air slowly upwards until his lungs emptied and his head began to roar.

Surfacing in a cascade of bath water, heaving for breath, he opened his eyes and saw the boots and uniformed legs standing above him at the edge of the bath. Blinking his eyes free of water, he lay back and saw the shaven head of the Chief, the heavy moustache and the crafty eyes surrounded by seams of fat that merged into jowls on either side of the Chief Officer's broken nose.

'Well?' the Governor snapped, his voice testy and irritable through having the peace of his bath disturbed.

'There are things I do not like, happenings I do not understand.' The Chief picked up a large towelling square, held it open so that the 'V' insignia could be seen like a flag displayed in a parade. The invitation to quit the water was obvious.

Groaning inside, the Governor climbed up the steps of the bath, and walked into the envelopment of the waiting towel.

'Drink, Chief.' He indicated the flagon of Emsidium wine.

The Chief grunted a note of thanks and lifted another glass and poured lavishly. Interesting, thought the Governor, that a second glass was set out almost as if Sevrin knew the Chief would be paying an 'unexpected' visit. Watch him, watch them, watch everybody, the Governor cautioned himself. Fiercely loyal to the system of Varos, he knew also that some of his ideas, unformulated as they were, aroused suspicion in the older officers. There had been secret assassinations, rigged votes, coups; well, best beware. The Governor watched the Chief drain his glass as if drinking nothing better than a drought of brackish recycled water.

'What is it, Chief? My day's work is completed.'

'We cannot open the spaceship of the intruders. It resists our strongest cutting bits; even the granite churners blunt and burn out.'

'But the owner, the man in the strangely-coloured coat. He is dead?'

'Oh, yes, he has been taken to the mortuary to await disposal first thing in the morning.'

'Then it doesn't matter does it?'

'No, except that Quillam has shown an interest in examining the stranger's spaceship.'

'Ah.' Now the Governor understood. The Chief Officer and the designer of Dome technology were old and bitter enemies. Each occupying permanent powerful positions, they hated and plotted against each other in a constant battle to frustrate the progress and success of the other in any way, no matter how trivial.

'Why not let him have it?' the Governor suggested mischievously.

'Sir!' The bald pate flushed angrily at the suggestion.

'But you can do nothing with it . . .'

'There is a way . . . there was a girl with the intruder. She would know how to enter the ship, wouldn't she?'

'Probably.' The Governor wanted his dinner, wanted to view the latest video recordings sent from Taza, the entertainment capital of his galaxy. There was a latest Bindo Banji comedy and the thought of being drawn into yet another internal wrangle between chiefs was too much to bear or contemplate.

'Have I your permission to interrogate the girl before Quillam grabs her, sir?'

Tired as the Governor was, an alarm sounded somewhere in his brain. 'Yes. But in my presence . . . tomorrow.'

'But . . .'

'Enough, Chief. We will deal with tomorrow's events tomorrow.'

'Sir, negotiator Sil demands an audience.'

61

'Tomorrow,' the Governor insisted.

'We . . .'

'Good night, Chief.' Centuries of authority crackled through that simple dismissive sentence. Despite himself, the Chief reacted and automatically saluted.

'Tomorrow then, sir.'

Scowling, the Chief strode away, leaving the Governor sipping his glass of blue wine and pleased at having for once bested the Chief in a battle of priorities.

Peri huddled next to the sleeping bodies of Areta and Jondar for warmth in the bleak cell within the punishment cell block, letting her thoughts wander through the crazy frantic events of the day. She wondered about the fate of the Doctor. Probably he had escaped and was even now working towards them to effect a rescue. She found the thought comforting. Resting her head on Areta's back, she drifted away into a fitful sleep while the guards patrolled outside and the suffering within the Punishment Dome was tempered by the nightly shutdown of the cameras that would activate again with the new day, ready to transmit each new torment of the prisoners.

Grumbling and moaning, the two mortuary attendants Az and Oza sorted through the day's intake of dead bodies. The curly-haired Doctor attracted their attention through his gaudy apparel but a search through his pockets revealed nothing of value.

'Someone got there first,' the cadaverous one called. Oza turned to his companion, the rodent-faced Az, who grimaced at his fellow worker. 'Retrieval squad's been through all these stiffs. Nothing left to steal here.'

'Should we acid-bath them now?' Az indicated the sprawled heaped bodies, grotesque in the careless tumble of death.

'Nah. The acid wants changing, do it tomorrow.'

'Right.' Oza wiped his hands down his uniform trousers then walked over to the doorway using the Doctor's chest as a convenient step along the way.

'Anyhow– ' Az nodded up to the dead eye of the camera that was placed high up in a corner of the stone mortuary– 'We might get featured in some pictures of the acid burnin' if there's nothin' else happenin' tomorrow.'

'Does that mean a bonus on our wages?' Oza asked eagerly, his yellowed fang teeth protruding as if to fasten onto a morsel.

'Yeh. Half a credit if you're on screen more than a minute.' Oza's grin widened.

'Then we'll lower these bodies ever so gently into the acid-bath, won't we?'

'Oh, ever so slowly.' Az cackled back at his partner as they went out into the corridor, locking the mortuary door and leaving the dead behind them.

Etta lay beside her snoring husband Arak and wished she could go to sleep. The ceiling of their tiny sleeping cell became a screen for her mind's eye and on it she projected the face of the fair-haired stranger who had perished earlier that evening.

'Oh, what's the matter with me?' Etta sighed restlessly. 'Good job Pol Corps can't see inside my head . . .'

'They can . . .' Arak muttered in gruff reply. For a mad moment Etta thought it might be true. A cold shiver scuttled through her before she jabbed her pointed little elbow into her husband's side in retaliation for the scare he had given her.

'Ow! What was that for?'

'To wish you good night, dear,' said Etta and turned her back on him.

*　　　*　　　*

63

Scanning his monitor screens on closedown Bax saw nothing worth recording. Everyone in the Punishment Dome was either sleeping or dead. The thought made Bax check the mortuary. On the screen the stone slabs near the acid-bath were stark and empty. Typically the slovenly attendants had just dumped the corpses any old how on the floor. Bax made a mental note to check that the bodies were displayed fully tomorrow; the viewers would want to see the curly-haired intruder in his coat of many colours one more time before the corrosive acid destroyed his body completely.

9

Interrogation

The following morning Peri found herself shaken roughly awake and pushed out of the cell she had shared with Areta and Jondar.

'Where are you taking me?' she demanded of the surly black-suited guards.

'The Governor' was all the explanation she received before she was bundled into a patrol car.

There then began a monorail journey from the main Punishment Dome to the separate dome of the communications centre that contained the nerve centre of the video spy system and the office of the Governor.

Strapped into her seat, Peri blinked as the light through the porthole by her head changed from the gloom of the Punishment Dome to the harsh glare of light reflected from the rocky red terrain of Varos. There seemed a complete absence of life outside the enclosed transparent tube in which the patrol car was now gliding smoothly. Peri focused through the porthole trying to divert her mind from dwelling on what might be waiting for her at the end of the journey. Dotted around the undulating landscape she could see the smooth bubbles of other domes that must, she presumed, protect the unfortunates who struggled to exist on this forbidding world. The unyielding unchanging aspect soon began to oppress Peri so that it was almost a relief when the patrol car finally clicked into a docking gate in the main government dome.

Escorted by her guards, Peri climbed the metal steps and ducked through an oval entrance and into the outer circle of the dome interior. Winding around as far as she could see was a long line of forlorn women dressed in dull shapeless clothes shuffling along at less than a snail's pace. The sight was so odd that Peri stopped and glanced questioningly at the guard to her left.

'What are they queuing for?'

'Ration of food.'

'Half-rations, more like,' his companion added with bitterness.

'But . . .' Peri began, quite failing to understand why a planet so blessed with the precious resource of Zeiton-7 should be anything but prosperous.

'Just shut up. You'll be given plenty of chances to talk soon. In fact, you'll be positively encouraged to.'

The guards said no more but nudged each other and glanced at their apprehensive prisoner without pity or compassion.

Scanning around the Punishment Dome through the lenses of his 207 video cameras, Bax considered what best to offer the early morning viewers of Varos. Something uplifting to start the day such as the disposal of yesterday's star turn, the red-coated figure now just visible on the mortuary floor. Bax flipped a microphone switch that gave him access to the attendant's workspace. 'I wish to transmit pictures of acid disposal procedure. Start with one corpse then make something special of that fair-haired body in the patchwork coat. I will be featuring his dissolution so make sure no clumsy mistakes occur.'

The blue 'Instructions received' light blinked back at him and Bax brought up another scene from the Punishment Dome to act as a filler spot. Bax monitored a small group of bedraggled wretches who scavenged a precarious living from feeding on their less fortunate fellow prisoners. It was familiar viewing watching the almost naked virtually sub-human creatures gnawing and sucking on bones with little trace of the repugnance they might have once felt for their condition. Disgusting Bax thought, but he held the group in mid close-up anyway. Showing such scenes would caution the viewers about what might happen to them should they be foolish enough to deviate from the rules by which Varosian society functioned.

A sound of marching feet behind made Bax swivel around angrily in his chair.

'You are not to disturb . . .' he began, then saw the slight blue figure dwarfed by the black-uniformed guards who surrounded her. 'Ah. The prisoner for interrogation. I will alert the Governor.' Bax pressed an entry switch and waited for the door of the adjoining office to slide open.

Expecting to see the Governor, Bax was surprised instead by the sight of a squat green figure being carried forth. One glance was enough to show that the Galatron negotiator was very angry indeed.

'How dare you interrupt my bargaining? You have quite disturbed the concentrated thinkings of your Governor!'

'It's all right, Bax . . .' The Governor had followed the irate Thoros-Betan and his two burly dark-skinned bearers into the communications centre. 'Delegate Sil has heard enough this morning to realise we still have far to go before a conclusion is reached about the price of Zeiton ore.'

'I might have but you do not have far to go, Governor! Your people do not approve your actions. They do not like your strategies, they do not like *you*!' That thought changed the irate green creature's mood and he began to cackle with what, for him, passed as mirth. His stunted slug-like body shook while his sting lifted and pulsated with the gurgles that racked his plated chest. 'Soon your voters will say enough, away with him. No money for food, no Governor!'

Sil began to choke and cackle wildly once again. Knowing that what Sil said was true, the Governor made himself suppress further thought about the matter and turned instead to the task of unravelling the puzzle of yesterday's intruders and the problem of obtaining entry into their mysterious spacecraft. Making himself relax, he walked across to the guards and the girl. Placing a slight smile on his lips that he hoped would convey confidence, even friendliness, he asked gently, 'What is your name?'

'What's yours?' Peri said defiantly, though inside she felt only panic and apprehension.

'I have no name since I became Governor.'

Peri thought that the Doctor too possessed no other name. Out of the corner of her eye she noticed a flash of colour on the main screen of the monitors. Peri stared closely, hardly believing what she saw. An anguished cry of surprise leapt from her throat and with a speed that surprised everyone she darted towards the monitor screens and Bax, who had just switched to the stillness of the mortuary where the attendants Oza and Az were raising cadavers onto slabs including the body of the Doctor.

'Doctor, what . . . what's happened to you?' Peri whispered. Bax flicked up a big close-up of the Doctor's waxen face.

'You animals . . . what have you done to the Doctor!' Peri wailed and turned to attack the Governor who, though surprised, easily contained the onslaught of the frantic grief-stricken girl.

'Surely it is obvious your companion is dead.' The Governor spoke calmly and without trace of comfort in his voice. Death was a fact here and seemed hardly worthy of further comment. For Peri it was a different matter. Her manner distraught, her voice hardly able to contain her grief, Peri made herself turn back to the screen. 'Not the Doctor. I don't believe – can't believe – he's dead . . . no!'

'But he is. As you see.' The Governor's voice was cool and firm.

'You did it!' the girl's anguish turned to anger against the tall fair-haired man beside her.

'Not really. This Doctor had the hallucination that he was lost in a desert, his mind thought he was dying of thirst . . .'

'His body agreed,' Sil cut in, '. . . so die they did!' The volley of mad laughter filled the communications centre as Sil reacted to his own brand of callous humour. Peri watched as Sil teetered precariously on the edge of his tank, then shook her head to clear the nightmare scene; but the sombre guards, the crazy cackling green creature, the grim bearers, Bax, the Governor in his grey serge uniform remained all too real to her eyes as did the unmoving image of the Doctor still in close-up on the central monitor screen.

Peri's gaze switched back to Sil. 'What is . . . is that . . . that thing?'

'Show respect!' the nearest guard warned.

'It's all right . . .' the Governor motioned the guard away. 'You said your companion was called the Doctor?'

'Yes.'

'And what is your name?'

Peri didn't want to give this strange brutal assembly anything of herself but then the little green angry object quivering on its water tank screamed out at her with awful and frightening force. 'Answer! Answer! *Answer!*'

'Peri . . .' Inadvertently the name spilled out.

'Why are you here, Peri?' the Governor said in gentle firm enquiry that in its own way was as disconcerting as the wild demand that Sil had terrified her with moments before.

'You . . . you wouldn't believe me if I told you . . .' Peri faltered.

The Governor's hand took her arm and guided her towards his office.

'I promise I will listen to your story, Peri, however fantastic you may think it to be.'

'I . . .' Before Peri could finish, her eye caught movement on the main screen. For a wild second hope surged through her that the Doctor lived but it was only the mortuary attendants shifting him aside to allow them to reach another corpse that they then began to bear towards the waiting acid-bath that sizzled and hissed nearby.

'What are they doing?'

'Waste disposal. Sil grinned at the horrified realisation on the girl's face. 'Maybe we should show her the fate of those who meddle in the affairs of Varos, eh, Governor?'

The Governor shrugged. 'Why not?'

Frozen in a petrified fascination Peri watched the attendants pause by the edge of the acid-bath and begin to lower the unknown body towards the burning acid.

'No.' Peri turned her head away but a moment later a guard's strong hands wrenched it back again to force her to witness the dissolution of the body as it was consumed by the corrosive acid. For a second the skeleton of the unknown victim could be glimpsed; then that too disintegrated under the seething corrosion of the acid dissolution.

Sickened by the horror of what she had just witnessed Peri trembled and felt her hold on consciousness slipping fast.

'This way . . .' Peri felt herself guided from the chamber by the Governor and found herself taken tremblingly into the austere office that was dominated by the imposing desk and elaborate chair of governmental authority.

'We can talk here,' the Governor said, closing the door and regarding her intently.

Peri swayed groggily once more.

The Governor at last seemed to realise just how upset Peri was and, with a semblance of concern, began to talk soothingly about how safe she was with him, how he only wanted to help her. The not unpleasant voice lulled Peri . . . her eyes closed and she found herself drifting into a state of near stupor under the honeyed tones of the Governor.

'Rest . . . rest,' intoned the Governor, looking down upon the slim figure of the girl now slumped wearily against his office wall.

'Here, come and sit down.' Peri found herself taken across to the Governor's chair.

'Thanks.' Gratefully she settled into the high chair of office. The Governor looked at her strangely. 'What . . . what is it?'

'Nothing. You look so small . . . so vulnerable that's all . . .'

'We'll see,' said the Governor, glancing up above the chair where the beams of pain or pleasure were waiting to descend on the chair's victim should he decide to engage the chair's interrogation mode on the helpless girl. That could be used later, he thought. 'Rest. Take your time. Recover from the death of your companion.'

'Thanks.'

'Not at all.'

'Seen all this before.' Arak yawned as he pushed back his chair from the small bare breakfast table where he had shared a meagre unappetising breakfast of gruel with his wife.

'What?' Etta said absently wondering what the one

71

label-less can remaining on her kitchen shelves might contain.

'This acid-bath stuff.' Arak gestured towards the screen. 'Always the same . . . seen one stiff meltin' down, seen 'em all . . .'

'Oh, suppose so . . .' Etta glanced absently at the screen, then frowned alertly.

'What is it, Etta?'

'I thought the dead one, him in the red coat, I thought he moved.'

'Reflex.'

'This long after? No.'

They both stared at the screen with renewed interest as Oza and Az prepared to lift the Doctor towards his final obliteration by immersion in the sizzling acid-bath.

In the mortuary Az and Oza were conscious that the eyes of Varos were upon them. In careful unison they timed their approach, Oza to the head and shoulders, Az to the feet of the Doctor.

'Lift . . .' Oza whispered and bent over the Doctor's face. Suddenly a steel blue eye opened with a mischievous twinkle.

'I've had the most peculiar dream,' the Doctor said conversationally and yawned up into Oza's face, sending the mortuary attendant reeling back towards the acid-bath under the shock of the Doctor's sudden return from the ranks of the dead.

'Well, can't stay,' said the Doctor cheerfully and swung his legs down from the mortuary slab. 'Ooh, bit chilly in here . . .' Then rubbing his hands, he stepped adroitly out of the way of the concerted rush of Az and Oza from either side of him.

The attendants bellowed as they collided with each other then turned towards the Doctor who now innocently loitered near the streaming, hissing acid-bath.

'Quite corrosive, I would have thought,' the Doctor said conversationally.

'Yeh. An' you're about to find out just how much!' Az yelled and launched himself at the Doctor who, hoping for just this wild rush, stepped nimbly aside causing the attendant to crash into the side of the bath, teeter for a moment then overbalance with the force of his assault.

'Aaaahh!' The yell stopped abruptly then resumed as the frantic attendant flailed desperately to obtain a footing so as to clamber clear of the burning, scalding acid-bath.

'Help me!' he yelled, panic-stricken.

'Hold on!' his companion dashed to his partner's rescue extending a helping hand that was grabbed with urgent haste exerting such force through blind panic that the unfortunate rescuer toppled on top of Az. Both submerged under the surface of the very acid-bath into which they had lowered thousands of victims of the Punishment Dome.

'Dear . . . dear . . .' The Doctor shook his head sadly as he contemplated the effects of the painful immersion that the attendants had callously planned for him. An arm thrashed around. A head surfaced but soon the acid had done its work and the Doctor, realising that nothing could have been done to save the unfortunate Oza and Az let himself out into the corridor, determined to place some distance between himself and the mortuary where he was certain the cameras must have monitored his miraculous return to life.

'Boo . . . rubbish!'

Arak pointed at the screen where the white bones of the unfortunate guards could just be seen in the seething disposal vat.

'It's a fix!'

'That's real acid,' Etta said, her eyes never wavering from the process of dissolution now in close-up on the screen.

'Never,' said Arak but his voice faltered uncertainly as he failed to figure out how the rulers of Varos had staged their latest piece of trickery.

'Renegade escaped,' Etta wrote neatly on her report then looked up at her husband. 'That rebel in the patchwork coat has now equalled the survival record.'

'It's all fixed . . . all of it,' Arak muttered but his former certainty was no longer as apparent as before. Thoughtfully he looked at the screen where no sign of the guards could now be seen apart from the odd cluster of bubbles that occasionally disturbed the surface.

'I wonder what's going on?' he said.

'We'll see,' said Etta as she turned to a new viewstat report sheet.

'I wonder if that guy in the red coat could be the one to survive the Dome and find the escape panel on the other side?'

This time Etta was the one to express derision.

'No one could ever be that good or that lucky.'

'No . . . no . . . not that I believe such an exit exists . . . even if anyone got right through the dangers of the Dome the officers would still be waiting. Yeah, it's all a big fix . . . all of it.' Then Arak sighed and turned away from the screen, saddened that in his dark conception of the world of Varos no one could ever win.

Slowly and stiffly the Doctor groped his way down an unlit passageway. The Doctor's whole Gallifreyan metabolism after the excitement of his escape from the attentions of Az and Oza felt sluggish and out of sorts. Obviously the decision he had taken to feign death in order to combat the power of the 'desert storm' had taken a great toll of his lifeforce. To suspend animation by stopping one of his hearts completely and to go into low hibernation pulse with the other was as dangerous an exercise as he had always been told it was.

Not to be recommended, the Doctor thought, as he groped his way along the gloomy corridor that led away from the mortuary. His mind gradually cleared and turned from past dangers to the necessity of discovering the present whereabouts of Peri.

10

Quillam

'I can't believe the Doctor is no more,' Peri said in a small voice, wiping away her tears.

'Oh, yes, of course. You grieve for his death . . .' The Governor frowned at his oversight. 'I forget that people do.'

'*You* don't?'

'I might have done once but now death is my only friend, my constant and loving companion.' A shrug and a wave of his hand encompassed the cold cheerless office. 'Can you feel his presence, Peri?'

A shiver passed through the girl seated in the Governor's chair. 'I don't want to, thanks.'

'Well, you should; seeing that at this very moment your life is even more at risk than mine.'

Peri sensed the questioning was about to begin for the Governor's blue eyes narrowed and focused upon her; but just as he was about to phrase his first question the door opened and the shaven head of the Chief Officer appeared.

'Sir . . .'

'I said, no interruptions . . .'

'That Doctor . . . he's escaped.'

The Governor glanced at Peri who stared in disbelief at the Chief Officer.

'It's a trick . . .' she said eventually, making herself suppress the hope that had surged and warmed her being with its brief presence.

'Yes, on us. He was only pretending to be dead though all physical checks showed no sign of life.'

'He's alive then?' The small spark of hope glowed again within her.

'And running. He's got clear, sir.'

'Good . . .' The Governor nodded decisively.

'Good, sir?' The Chief did not understand.

'Recapture him . . .' the Governor explained patiently. 'Then we can bargain this girl's life for information from our mysterious Doctor friend.'

'Ah.' The Chief smiled. 'I'll arrange that straight away.'

A cruel self-satisfied smile played upon the Governor's mouth, an expression that goaded Peri into furious attack.

'I thought maybe you were a bit better than those other brutes!'

The Governor smiled at her anger.

'Sorry.'

Then he shrugged, turned and left the girl who stared ahead before starting to rise, a movement that activated the restraining clamps on the arms of the chair which closed about her wrists with a sudden and painful snap. Fear gave her a manic energy but try as she might Peri could not budge the steel restraining bands until, finally wearied, she sank back into a hopeless stupor and waited dully for the next wave of horror to engulf her.

The Governor, the Chief Officer and Bax conferred worriedly before the bank of screens that showed the many variations of cruelty being practised throughout the Punishment Dome.

'Where is the Doctor?' the Chief demanded and scanned the screen furiously.

'Not in sight of our cameras.'

'Try again!' the Chief urged Bax. 'We must locate him.'

'I've scanned through twice, sir.'

'Why isn't he within reach of our cameras? We cover every section of our jurisdiction . . .'

Bax shifted uncomfortably. 'I've checked a ground plan. He could have followed an old linking passage and gone into the inner prison control centre.'

Inadvertently Governor and Chief Officer glanced at each other, one name entering both of their thoughts at the same instant.

'Quillam?' The Chief breathed the name for both of them.

'He refuses to allow our cameras to enter his domain, sir.'

'Then that's where this Doctor must have gone,' the Governor spoke decisively.

'But our guards can't enter without Quillam's permission.'

'Then request it, Chief. I must have the Doctor captured. I must discover who he is and what is his reason for being on Varos. Without this information I am at a complete disadvantage in my negotiations with Sil. Go, attend to it!'

'Sir.'

Watching the Chief hurry away, Bax ventured a question.

'Quillam has beamed messages about the Doctor, sir. Seems he's been monitoring his escapes and doesn't approve of our tactics.'

The Governor frowned. 'Whatever we do will never be enough for Mr Quillam. He wishes he was Governor instead of head of prison control and interrogative research. Only one thing prevents him, the thought that if he did not win favour with the people he would be required to pay for their disfavour with his life. So he lurks in his control centre like a slug under a stone!'

'Yes, sir,' was all Bax thought it wise to say in reply, given the obvious anger of the Governor at the mention of

78

his hated rival's name. Tactfully, he turned back to his screens and began to close in on the mortuary scene where two rather squeamish prison guards were being instructed about their disposal duties as replacement attendants for the luckless Oza and Az.

Contemplating yet another pair of musty passages ahead, the Doctor wondered why as yet there had been no pursuit of him. Scanning the crumbling walls no devices or beams signifying punishment zones could be seen. Indecisively, the Doctor turned first in one direction then the other as he contemplated the junction of corridors. One fork had dust on its floor long undisturbed while away down the other tunnel a monorail glinted dully under the faint glow of the minimal illumination given by working lights.

A distant sound came to the Doctor's attention. It was a low vibrating hum as if from a distant power source.

Anxious to make contact with someone or something that might lead him to Peri, the Doctor opted to follow the monorail that he hoped would lead to the cause of the low whirring sound.

The jarring whine became louder and louder and soon the Doctor realised that he was walking along a passage that led towards what must be the main passageway of . . . of what? The lights were now becoming brighter as the Doctor reached the conjunction of two further corridors. Cautiously he peered around the corner, a fortunate precaution for almost upon him came two technicians deep in a conversation that held their attention enough to allow the Doctor to dodge back unseen, praying at the same time that the pair would not take a sharp left turn into his exposed hiding place. Thankfully the Doctor heard their voices recede but what they were talking about seemed to be worthy of further investigation. What they were discussing was a rather crude formulation that could, with development, lead to advanced nuclear fission techniques. Can't have that, the Doctor decided, and began to follow the two white-coated technicians along the main passageway.

The pair, still engrossed, turned into a wider chamber and disappeared through steel-clad doors that displayed, in blood red letters, the warning *Entrance forbidden. Authorised personnel only.*

To the Doctor such notices always beckoned and this instance was to be no exception to his usual practice.

Pushing the doors open only revealed another pair of doors with round observation windows. Peering in, the Doctor surveyed a large cavernous space packed with transmitters, transformers, and further enclosed chambers that must, the Doctor guessed, contain technology to harness the power to give energy to the whole Punishment Dome.

Seated before monitoring units were some dozen workers. Chief amongst them facing a TV screen sat a figure whose features were completely hidden from view by the grey plastic mask that gave his appearance a chilling effect, as if the prison control centre had at its head a cold calculating automaton.

The Doctor pushed the doors ajar, anxious to glimpse the details of the clicking, hissing, pulsating technology that must monitor and control all the intricate zones and devices of the hellish region at whose heart he now found himself.

With his opening of the door he strained to hear the words of the masked figure as it pushed away from the control chair at the centre of web of cruelty that had trapped and claimed the lives and reason of so many victims.

On seeing the two technicians who had come to report for their shift, Quillam stood stiffly.

'We must be aware that there is a fugitive loose, perhaps in our sector. Be alert.'

The technicians nodded and took their places in the nerve centre of the complex network of instrumentation.

Quillam began to walk with an uneven limping gait towards the exit doors. Fortunately his slowness of movement allowed the Doctor to retreat back into the corridor. Glancing up and down, the Doctor saw that no matter how quickly he could run in any direction he was bound to be seen by the man in the mask now moving towards him. Hurrying away, the Doctor frantically searched for a hiding place, then saw a closed door. He tried the handle, the door opened and the Doctor found himself in a small room obviously used to store protective clothing; on the rack opposite him hung several white coats and a grey plastic mask, the twin of that worn by the man whose exit from the control chamber had forced the Doctor to retreat.

Rapidly the Doctor took down a coat, put it on and picked up the grey mask, clapped it to his face, pulled together the narrow adhesive contact strip that held it in place and turned anxiously towards the door, hoping that his disguise would not need to be tested too thoroughly.

After a few seconds and just when the Doctor began to think he was not to be discovered, he saw the handle turn and the door start to open. Quillam entered, stopped, surprised at the sight of someone who could have been an exact double of himself; recovering quickly, Quillam reached into the pocket of his uniform for the phaser weapon he always carried. The Doctor spoke first as both masked figures regarded each other tensely.

'Hello. I thought you were my mirror image . . . until I realised I wasn't holding a gun.'

'A very effective energy weapon that could vaporise you instantly.'

'Which would only leave one of us.'

'Who are you?'

The Doctor bowed slightly.

81

'A student of science. Much interested in primitive technology.'

'Primitive . . .' Quillam started as if insulted then controlled his reaction. 'The mask . . . remove it.'

Seeing his double adjust the phaser weapon control slide to maximum force made the Doctor decide to comply. With the mask removed the air of the chamber felt cool to his sweating face. Quillam watched the Doctor wipe away beads of perspiration.

'I've seen you on the video screens . . . you've recently returned from the dead.'

'A rather refreshing suspension of animation, actually,' the Doctor smiled, but the eerie mask revealed nothing though the eyes of Quillam stared with a malevolent gleam of hostility while the Doctor continued. 'Hardly worth the effort. No doubt there'll be something novel arranged so that I can return to being *kaputt* in the most dramatic fashion.'

The phaser weapon waved slightly in a gesture of casual agreement.

'I expect something might be arranged. 'Why don't we have a word with the executioners They're always on the look-out for fresh victims to practise their art upon.'

The gun waved again this time indicating the Doctor should leave the room ahead of Quillam.

'No, after you,' the Doctor said with mock politeness.

'I don't think so,' came the flat humourless reply.

There was nothing for it but to obey. Grimly the Doctor moved towards the door wondering what bizarre ritual he was to be forced to participate in next.

11

Condemned

The delegate of the Galaton Mining Company pointed a stubby green finger at the terrified girl trapped in the Governor's chair and demanded shrilly, 'Why is she on Varos?'

'She won't say,' the Governor reiterated patiently.

Sil's features contorted with the effort of remaining in control of his anger and growing suspicion that Peri must be a secret agent of a rival mining corporation after the rare commodity of Zeiton-7.

Sil's next words, shrilled and distorted by the voice box translator, whined into Peri's hearing. 'Are you an employed agent of other mining companies. You and that man who was dead?'

Peri shook her head violently from side to side. Her hands chaffing and rubbing against the steel bands that held her wrists captive.

'No . . . no . . . I told you!'

'Liar!' Sil screamed. 'Liar! You belong to Amorb, you lying liar!'

The Governor, puzzled at Sil's insistence about this line of enquiry, asked the negotiator why Peri should be an agent of another mining corporation.

Filled with rage and apprehension, all the green slug-like creature could do in reply was to splutter and cackle and pretend that his anxiety and rage had overcome the circuits of his voice box's ablity to translate his reply.

Peri, desperate to escape the probing questions of the

Governor and the savage intensity of Sil, began to speak with a sincere and hopeless anguish.

'I'm from another time . . . another century . . . Nearly three hundred years before you were born I lived on another world.'

The Governor glanced quizzically to the Chief who had been observing the interrogation without, as yet, taking part.

'That's a new one.' The Chief grinned at the preposterous theory.

Peri went limp at the expression she saw on the faces before her. 'I had an idea you wouldn't believe me.'

'You were right,' the Governor spoke curtly. His patience had reached an end.

'What is it?' He turned to Bax as the technician hurried into the office.

Bax whispered his news while the Chief and Sil strained to catch word of what must be a significant new development given his urgency.

The Governor considered the message whispered to him while regarding Peri thoughtfully. In the lengthening silence the Chief ventured a solution.

'Sir, let's give her to the rehabilitators. Disturbance of her molecular structure will make her scream out the truth.'

Sil launched his cackling travesty of laughter in support of his secret ally.

'Put her into the reshapement chamber. We can watch her change into a beast or a birdie.' The obscene parody of humour gurgled out once again.

Peri didn't know what they were talking about but was certain that the refinement of horror mentioned must entail humiliation and suffering if something like Sil could find amusement in its contemplation.

Still the Governor did not speak. Sil's gurglings and splutterings finally ceased and, after a moment's silence the blonde-haired leader of Varos enquired almost gently, 'Why are you here, Peri? Tell us, please.'

That word 'please', so often heard and used by Peri in another life, another time, triggered a response that mixed sincerity with an anguished appeal for help and understanding. Straining against the steel bracelets that clamped her arms to the Governor's chair of office, blinking away tears of helplessness, she began a further plea.

'All right: our TARDIS . . . that box outside is, if you like, a ship of time, a sort of spacecraft and . . . oh, I don't understand the technical stuff . . . but the Doctor said we must have this special metal to fix the bearings or something so we had to come here . . . so . . . so . . . that's what we did.'

Peri's words petered away as she saw the unrelenting disbelief on the set angry faces before her.

Sil scowled. 'She's laughing at us all over the face!'

'I've told you the truth! Don't you recognise the sound any more!' Peri heard her voice rise into a squeal of hysteria.

'We're getting nowhere with this stupid girl, sir.'

The Chief turned to the Governor.

'No matter. Once again we have captured the mysterious Doctor. Quillam came across him at prison control.'

'He'd like that, sir.'

'Yes.' The Governor became thoughtful, trying to balance the factors of the strange situation with the need to feed the craving of the Varosian people for ever more violent spectacle.

'How long is it since we rigged an old style execution?'

Frowning, the Chief recalled a whole gruesome parade of televised executions. 'Not since the Outer Dome sabotage trial. Months ago.'

'Then I think it's time we staged another, Chief.'

A chuckle sounded in the throat of the Chief Officer. 'They're always enjoyable aren't they, sir?'

Watching the anticipation of the quartet before her all exchanging glances of spiteful relish filled Peri with chilling unbelief at what she was forced to witness. 'What kind of vermin are you?' she demanded.

'Vermin who will watch your deathing throes with much joy, my dearest!' Sil laughed delightedly as he watched the Varosian leaders begin to issue instructions for the arrangements for an execution that was bound to cheer a creature like him with its barbarity.

The video camera that monitored the actions of the inmates of the Punishment Dome showed nothing new: just a close shot of some ragged wretches gnawing at a bone scavenged from a decaying heap of garbage they were supposed to be sifting. Etta dutifully monitored the close-up on her view-stat report while, across their living cell, Arak dozed noisily in a chair before the large flickering wall screen.

'Woh? Uh . . . oh . . . mm?' Arak came awake, as he usually did, full of vague foreboding. Blearily he blinked and stared around the familiar sparse furnishing of his home-cell. Finally he stared at his wife who, absorbed in making yesterday's viewing report, paid him scant attention.

'What you doing?'

'Viewer's report of domestic verbal reaction.'

A lurch of alarm passed through Arak. 'I'm not on it, am I?' Yesterday if I said anything about anything it was only because I was tired.'

Etta looked at him and smiled enigmatically, enjoying the power her DVR reports gave her in their marriage battles. Arak glared at his wife. 'Reports, spying. Working men should be . . .' The rapid movement of Etta's pen made him halt his complaint abruptly.

'Yes?' Etta prompted, her pen poised to note down

his next complaining remark. Arak realised a rapid change of tack was necessary.

'Er, working men not, er, taken seriously for the rubbish they might have spoken earlier.'

Etta smiled triumphantly, her role of dominance over her man established nicely for the rest of the night. Arak turned his resentment onto the screen which now showed a violent dispute over a well-gnawed bone. Watching the emaciated prisoners clawing and fighting weakly over the gruesome morsel irritated him.

'Do we have to watch this?' he demanded.

'Yes.'

'Always the same . . . Still, at least they've something to eat.'

'There'll be something good on screen soon.'

'Oh yeh? What?'

'You'll see,' said Etta who guessed the programme controllers must be planning a special event soon to inject some excitement into what had seemed very dull video viewing since the Doctor had escaped from the waiting acid-baths in the disposal chamber.

In the prison video central studio a wooden scaffold had been erected with practised ease. From the window of his cell the Doctor watched a black-hooded figure busily intent on testing each of the four nooses that dangled ominously over the drop that the trap doors covered. The varying weights were meticulously fastened to the hanging ropes and the trap doors were opened with a sickening clatter in the scaffold floor by means of a long wooden lever placed at the side of the wooden gibbet.

The Doctor turned away from the cell window, unable to witness the placing of the smallest weight that he knew represented the body mass of someone he feared must be Peri. Assuming a lightness of spirit he did not really feel, the Doctor tried to raise the morale of his companions.

'All very traditional. The whole ghastly hanging ritual to be played out fully by the look of it.'

Jondar came to the window and stared dully across what seemed to be the setting of a medieval courtyard complete with straw and even a wooden tumbril.

'A televised execution. Death by hanging.' Inadvertently Jondar's hand touched his throat.

'Three guesses whose necks they're after,' the Doctor said flippantly.

Jondar frowned. 'There's four nooses.'

Leaning against the wall nearest to the door of the cell Areta looked hopelessly ahead of her. 'A spare. They're very thorough.'

'The fourth rope is for Peri, I would have thought,' said the Doctor. 'But why isn't she with us?'

Jondar's eyes never wavered from the dangling ropes and the busy executioner. 'Plenty of other prisoners the authorities would be happy to rid themselves of,' he muttered gloomily.

'Why are they so anxious to eliminate you?' asked the Doctor. Jondar and Areta exchanged wry looks of knowledge mixed with bitter memory.

'Because I was curious,' Jondar began. 'Simply curious. Varos is airless. We live in artificial domes scattered about the surface of the planet. Movement between domes is impossible without official permission.'

'I can imagine.'

'Most Varosians live in poverty,' continued Areta, her voice dull with lack of hope. 'They work in the mines or in the video recording division, peddling real life death scenes for export to other worlds.' Jondar nodded then began answering the Doctor's question more fully.

'I used to maintain the surface shuttle cars. One day I

was required to deliver a shuttle car to the dome where the Chief Officer lives. Whenever I needed to collect cars I was never allowed into is domain. Security was excessive, even for Varos. Eventually my curiosity became too much. I hid inside a car that needed extensive repair; then, when the guards were changing shifts for the evening, I slipped inside, stayed just long enough to see into the dome, to see how the elite live. Luxury, richness, wealth . . .' The memory of the sights glimpsed so fleetingly dazed Jondar with their recall.

After a pause Areta continued the account quietly but with an intensity of hatred at the revelation of the rulers' cynical deception. 'Jondar didn't see much but just enough to realise that a giant deceit had taken place against our people, all the people, that is, except the favoured – the very favoured few.'

Jondar nodded. 'I took the first shuttle car I could find back to the main workpop dome but, just being absent that short time, twenty minutes late checking out on my shift, caused suspicion and eventually I was brought here . . .' Jondar's arm tightened around the shoulders of his wife and both of them turned to look out of the barred window to where the gallows waited.

'Without trial?'

'What's that?' Jondar asked, his voice dry with irony.

A key ground metallically in the lock of the cell door. The heavy wooden structure swung open to reveal the figure of a black-robed priest who held an open Bible reverentially before him. 'Good evening, my children,' the priest said gravely although he was hardly older than Areta and Jondar and a goodly number of centuries less than the Doctor.

The smooth-faced priest stepped aside to allow a stern overwarder to enter. 'Your appeal has been turned down,' the warder said gruffly, his manner stiff with formality. 'I am very sorry.'

'So should we have been had we bothered to make an

appeal,' said the Doctor cheerfully. Then addressing the cleric: 'Do you always play priest parts?'

A sharp look darted towards the Doctor but the priest decided to ignore the gibe and bent again over his holy book and began to lead the prisoners slowly out of the cell towards the waiting tumbril.

The Doctor took in the scene with a searching glance. Across the chamber, before the scaffold, stood a group comprising the Governor, the Chief, Sil with his attendants and another figure that stood next to the fearsome black-hooded executioner.

'Peri!'

'Doctor!'

Before they could take more than a step towards each other guards began to bind their hands behind them. Peri's plaintive voice called over: 'Doctor, I'm sorry. I've tried everything but they won't believe the truth!'

'Truth is a flexible commodity on Varos, Peri!'

Although the Doctor was pitching his voice across the chamber to Peri his eyes and thoughts were elsewhere, examining the camera positions that were tilting and focusing upon the centrepiece of the video-cast – the gibbet, the hangman and his ropes. Ah, yes, I see, he thought, then continued his interrupted conversation with Peri across the crowded chamber as he and Jondar were pushed onto the wooden tumbril and wheeled towards the Governor.

'So long as things *look* truthful that's quite sufficient for this lot here!'

The Governor, calm and suave as always stepped forward and faced the Doctor whose arms were now pinioned behind him. 'Enlighten us as to the truth about your unexpected visit, please, Doctor.'

The Doctor looked steadily down into the eyes of the Governor of Varos. 'To help Varos realise the wealth of her potential, what else?'

This reply galvanised Sil into a sneer that masked his sudden alarm.

'How? By eating rocks?' The maniacal laughter began to surge wildly. 'Tell us. Tell us! He doesn't know anything . . . do what we're here for – execute them!'

Under the cover of Sil's hysteria the Chief whispered to the Governor.

'This Doctor must have talked to Jondar and heard the lies.'

'Yes. Of course.' The Governor waved for his guards to bring the prisoners out of the cart then spoke with brisk authority. 'What is the staging plan?'

The Chief stood to attention. 'These two are to hang.' The jabbing forefinger of the Chief indicated the fate of the Doctor and Jondar.

'Very good. And the women?'

'I suggest they be given to the reshapement and cell mutation experiment, the results to be exhibited on our screens as a warning to women who support rebel husbands in acts of violation of the regulations of Varos.'

All eyes rested on the tall man in the grey uniform with the red, white and black sash of office.

'I confirm those sentences.'

The condemned Jondar held onto his composure with a great effort. As Areta was taken away the Chief could not resist adding to the burden of Jondar's despair.

'I'm sorry you will be denied the sight of the ladies turning into who knows what – a serpent, a griffin, a new admixture of fish and fowl.' The Chief grinned sadistically. 'Take the women away.'

The Governor glanced expectantly at the impassive face of the Doctor.

'Anything to add, Doctor? Anything that might persuade me to halt the sequence of events?'

'One request?'

This was what the Govenor and Chief wanted, a blurting-out of truth and pleading for mercy in exchange for information. 'One last request. Yes?' the Chief prompted.

'Well?' the Governor added after a moment.

The Doctor inclined his head towards Sil. 'Who is he? Why is something like that resident here?'

Surprised, Sil spluttered out a reply.

'What interest can my . . .' he began but the Governor interrupted briskly.

'The delegate from the Galatron Mining Corporation is visiting us to bargain over our yearly contract and review our market prices for the ore of Varos.'

'*Zeiton* ore? Zeiton-7 . . .' The Doctor's surprise quickened his speech, despite his effort to remain unmoved by the dangerous scenario in which he was cast as a leading player.

'That's all we have to sell of any value.'

The Governor waited for the strange visitor to say something further but the Doctor seemed lost in his own thoughts once again.

'I see. Thank you,' the Doctor mumbled, then lapsed into an even deeper abstraction of thought.

'Is that all you wish to know?' Puzzlement was apparent in the Governor's question but all the Doctor said was 'Mmm, for the moment.'

Sil decided the tension of the execution was flagging. 'A moment is all you have, Doctor. Take them to the scaffold. Playing for time of life is all they ever do!' Sil glared at the Chief.

'At once!' The Chief nodded and the Governor did nothing to stop the prisoners being taken towards the scaffold.

Jondar and the Doctor found themselves bustled up the steps and given into the arms of the burly executioner who pushed them carefully onto their respective trap doors before placing a knotted noose around each of their necks.

Jondar felt the trap beneath his feet tremble under his weight, felt the pressure of the rope constrict his larynx. Across the chamber, the woman he loved and the unfortunate Peri were being taken away. Areta looked back once, then was pushed out of his sight for ever. Jondar thought grimly that at least death would release him but for Areta and Peri there would soon be the ordeal of being condemned to inhabit bodies grotesquely and wilfully disfigured.

Jondar became aware that a stillness had come upon the chamber. The moment of death must be imminent. The eyes of the video cameras glinted coldly under the lights, all set, no doubt, to beam their death agonies and to give a fillip to mid-evening viewing within the homes of smug law-abiding Varosians.

'Anything to say, Doctor, anything that may yet save your lives?'

The Doctor seemed still deep in thought. 'Sorry?' The vague blue eyes blinked at the Governor standing below him.

'So am I, Doctor.' The Governor stepped back. From somewhere a roll of drums began; the Governor lifted a gloved hand and began to bring it down in a signal for the executioner to pull the lever that would open the trap doors to oblivion.

'Wait!'

The Governor relaxed, confident that his ploy had worked and that at last he would hear the truth about the visit to his planet by the mysterious Doctor. 'Hold on broadcast. No sound or vision!' His orders were addressed to the technicians and to the floor manager who controlled the recording of the video-cast.

The Doctor began to speak, his voice ringing out with resolute sincerity.

'My death will prevent Varos ever progressing out of the reach of extortion by such as the Galatron Mining Company. Our deaths will send the possibility of hope for

93

this planet back into the pit of misery and fear that has for so long been the lot of its poor people!'

Listening to this emotive address, Sil decided great danger to himself and his company was about to be done by this creature in the multi-coloured coat. Pushing his attendants towards the gallows, he screamed his orders: 'Pull the lever! Stretch them out of this life more than pronto!'

'Wait!' The Governor tried to halt the advance of Sil's attendants but they ignored him and continued purposefully towards where the executioner waited poised by the trap door release lever.

The Doctor spoke rapidly, racing against time.

'I came to Varos because I have a new source of energy supply. That which drives my TARDIS depends for its function on a rare and precious substance of Varos – Zeiton ore. My friends, I can show you new prosperity!'

Sil's screams became strident as his bodyguards finally reached the executioner. 'Kill! Kill! Kill! Destroy them, choke his mouth up, press that lever now!'

The strength of two strapping black attendants became too much for the executioner who was compelled to relinquish his grip on the scaffold lever.

Horrified, Jondar saw the muscles tighten in a black arm, the lever move and both his and the Doctor's trap doors opened simultaneously sending their bodies dropping down through the gibbet floor. Time went into distorted unreality for Jondar felt himself falling and falling while waiting for the agony of the final arrest that would sever his spine at the neck. Amazingly this did not happen, for the rope unbound itself from where it had been coiled on the spar above, allowing him to tumble onto staw-filled sacks below the gallows platform. Dazed by the shock of unexpected survival, Jondar peered into the darkness. Beside him, another body stirred and spoke in intense enquiry: 'Jondar, are you all right?'

Jondar tried to speak but at first no words would form

themselves into sound then, eventually: 'Yes . . . yes.'
The Doctor pressed Jondar's shoulder. Fumbling for
each other's aid they clambered to their feet, swaying
unsteadily on the uneven sacking that covered the floor.
Light darted in as a door was opened beside them. The
grinning face of a warder looked in.

'Care to rejoin the living?' he asked mockingly.

The Doctor stepped from beneath the gallows and
greeted the Governor with studied casualness. 'Do you
often employ that noose trick?'

'As a means of finding out true information it has often
been successful. You suspected our bluff?'

'I noticed your cameras weren't cabled to a power
point, yes.'

'Ah, most observant.'

'A real execution would at least have been recorded.'

'Yes. But you did make some interesting observations
while standing on the threshold of death, Doctor.'

'Did I?' Both watched each other searchingly.

The Governor stated flatly, 'I wish to know the truth
about your assertions.'

The Doctor stared stonily back at the ruler of Varos. 'I
will discuss nothing, reveal nothing, until I have evidence
that Peri and Areta have been released unharmed from
the transfiguration experiments. Until I see them . . .'

Before the Doctor could continue further Sil interrupted violently. 'He has nothing to reveal . . . he is
lying . . . he is an Amorb agent who wishes only to usurp
our worthy Galatron contracts with rashful promises!'

The Governor glanced at Sil then back to the Doctor,
his expressions in turn appraising and speculative.
Instinctively he felt that somewhere in the confused
situation lay advantage for Varos and himself; but who
could he trust? 'Until I can hear what each of you has to
say or, better still, offer, the matters raised here will not be
decided. Should you, Doctor, be lying, the next noose
about your neck will extend your spinal column past

breaking point.' The Governor turned a cold eye upon Sil. 'Should the Doctor be telling the truth about Zeiton ore and its potential, I would wish to know why Varos has been duped by you and your company these many years.'

The thought that perhaps the Governor was but a step away from the truth and that the Doctor might emerge victorious sent Sil into a tumult of rage. Thrashing about like a trapped tuna he spat out venomously, 'How dare I be spoken to like this! I reject all offers made . . .'

There was the advantage! The Governor spoke quickly. 'Thank you, Sil. That releases me from my people's decision that I must accept your latest terms.'

For Sil the situation was sinking from the bad to the catastrophic. The knowledge that he had blundered and would be held accountable to the unforgiving board of Galatron made the bile and gall of anger and fear swell like a geyser within him before finally erupting into a stream of steaming Thoros-Betan curses of such extreme force and potency that his translational voice box, in an effort to compensate went into terminal compression in its attempts to hold his wrath to manageable proportions. Then it gave up the struggle and exploded *zummtow*! on Sil's chest, releasing the pure sound of Thoros-Betan invective, a screeching assault on the hearing that made the squeal of chalk on blackboard melodious by comparison.

While everyone stood transfixed, only the Doctor seemed unaffected by the din made by the feral green slug screaming and splashing violently within its tank.

'I enjoy a cool debate, don't you, gentlemen?' he chuckled at those standing nearby in pained attitudes.

Resisting the desire to clap hands to his ears the Governor ordered tersely. 'Chief, have a new translational communicator brought from Sil's starship. Stop the transfigurational experiment on the women. That will give me the time I need to decide what the truth of all this is, and who may live and who must die.'

The Governor looked at all present in turn. A chill

descended on everyone as the understanding penetrated that the next sentence of death would be carried out without appeal or semblance of mercy.

12

The Changelings

The transmutation laboratory was painted a blinding white that reflected a beam, glittering with multifracted light, which swirled down from a NBD upon the bodies of Peri and Areta who lay strapped side by side to a table.

Peri strained to escape the intense light that played upon her. It was rather like an old style sunray lamp, she had thought in the brief pause when the technicians and their sinister masked controller had left them alone. That was before the particle bombardment had begun. But no simple infra-red rays would make her skin prickle and itch with such increasing discomfort so that she felt madness would soon come unless she could somehow gain relief.

'How long before – what d'you call it – transfiguration happens to us?' she gasped out to Areta, terrified.

'I heard that man in the mask say it was a matter for initial experiment.'

'That means anything could happen to us. Anything . . . They just want to turn this process onto us and see what happens!'

'Is anything happening?'

'I don't think so,' said Peri, squinting down as much as her bindings allowed. Then she realised what was happening and began to scream and scream.

'Peri!'

'My arms!' Peri sobbed up into the coloured fall of evil light. 'They're beginning to grow feathers, like a bird!'

Areta struggled to comfort her distressed comrade. 'Peri hold on . . . hold on!' So concerned was Areta for Peri that she was unaware that her own skin was beginning to scale and discolour towards a sickly green colour not dissimilar in shade to that of Sil.

The Chief waited until Sil was alone with only his attendants for company. His voice was still grating away interminably in unintelligible complaint.

'Here, use this for all our sakes.'

Muttering surlily, Sil took the new voice communicator box from the Chief Officer and plugged it into his speech connector necklace. Instantly his persistent whine turned into the somewhat eccentric English of the Thoros-Betan translation service.

'Intolerably improperly all of this that Doctor being allowed to even live!'

Patiently, the Chief explained their perilous position to his overwrought ally.

'Zeiton-7 has brought your company great wealth. You have miscalculated events. For the sake of paying a few miserable extra credits you may have lost the source of all our wealth and power.'

Sil became strangely quiet. In its way the sudden silence became menacing. The eyes of the Chief widened with alarm as he realised Sil's attendants were now heavily armed and that their HD phaser weapons were trained upon him.

'I have decided,' Sil spoke with haughty formality, 'to take over this planet of Varos. While you were fussing about finding a new voice box I was activating a coded distress signal that will bring, in forty-eight hours, a Galatron company force of acupuncture *correction* – [Sil's new voice box was a later model than used previously with a correcting device for the more obvious howlers.] – The *occupation* of this planet will help me to gain a little time to

99

allow the mercenaries arrival and I will spare you to assist in my annexation of this lump of reddy rock called Varos.'

With a wary eye on the attendants' guns the Chief Officer nodded his agreement.

Sil laughed delightedly. 'A wise decision, though you had little alternative to vaporisation, did you?'

'What if that Doctor tells the Governor what he suspects of the truth about how we have lied about the true worth of Zeiton ore?'

Sil thought for a moment then a gurgle of diabolical glee bubbled forth. 'He will not speak – *correction* – he will *only* speak if those female creatures are released unharmed.'

'Yes.'

'Have you done that, Chiefy?'

'Not yet.'

Again the demonic cackle gurgled in Sil's throat. 'Let us go and observate the experiment of the tissue transmo-grifier. I am most interested in the february of science – *correction* – *march* of science. So let us not impede its progress by stopping the experiment!' And again the manic glee spilled out of Sil and the Chief uneasily realised that the prospect of wielding power had given a new impetus to the already authoritarian Sil.

'Move!' Sil urged his attendants. 'Let us see what changes might have occurred to their bodies already.'

The attendants lifted Sil and carried their master out of the antechamber, following the Chief who led the way towards the section of the prison given over to the direct control of Quillam.

'I just won't look!' Peri said, clenching her eyes shut but feeling the stiff vulpine feathers that had now emerged almost fully all over her arms. Peri began to bear less and less resemblance to the attractive girl who, despite all her vicissitudes, had always retained a physical bloom of health. Now she had begun to resemble an ugly vulture-like bird with glossy black feathers that grew longer and longer as she approached final disfigurement.

Areta was a trifle more fortunate than Peri for she retained much of her original body shape though the texture of her skin had turned completely into a lizard-like scale of apple-green.

Outside the transmutation cell the Chief opened the observation hatch and stepped aside to allow Sil to be lifted up to view the scene within. An exclamation of delight issued from the alien, delight mixed with surprise at the sight of the distorted former human beings bound to a table, lit only by the glittering shower of radiation from the nuclear bombardment that they were undergoing.

'Doctor's friend is feathered fully.' Sil's eyes then darted to the green-scaled Areta. 'Ah, but the other female, she becomes ever and ever more attractive. How long before permanent result ensues?'

'Not too certain. This is an untried process.'

A new idea came to Sil. 'When I am Planetary Controller I will keep them both in my pleasure dome of pretty-pretty petlings!'

Sil giggled with much pleasure at the thought.

At the same time as Peri and Areta were being subjected to the experiment in the control room nearby Quillam was regarding the Governor, Doctor and Jondar with some amusement. The silence lengthened, only disturbed by the clickings, humming and flutterings of the monitoring panels that controlled the whole of the prison and Punishment Dome technology.

'Where are they?' Jondar demanded and took an impulsive step towards Quillam. Instantly two security

101

guards drew phasers from their belts and intervened, thrusting Jondar back to join the Doctor and the Governor as, at that moment the Chief joined them, pushing in through the swing doors that led into the prison control nerve centre.

'Well, where are they?' the Doctor asked.

The Chief Officer spread his hands apologetically. 'There's been a problem.'

'What?'

'The transmogrifier was at too advanced a stage. There was nothing we could do to reverse the transmutation. Sorry.'

The word 'sorry' accompanied by a small insincere smile on the fat lips of the Chief Officer propelled Jondar into reckless action. 'I'll kill you!' he shouted; but before his rush could carry him to the Chief the guards intervened and roughly pushed him away.

'Who is responsible for this process of mutation?' the Doctor demanded.

'I am,' said Quillam calmly and flicked a switch beside him that activated a screen which showed Peri and Areta now almost completely changed into creatures not formed by evolution but distorted, shaped by mysterious forces that even Quillam did not fully understand.

'Areta!' an agonised cry came from Jondar who turned away from the screen, unable to bear the sight of the green lizard that had once been Areta. Then, appealingly to the Doctor, he asked, 'Can't you do something?'

Quillam interrupted. 'There is nothing anyone can do. The process is probably too advanced.'

'Only probably?' the Doctor asked sharply.

'It is an unstable process.'

'The beam that radiates . . . what force of energy is it derived from?'

Quillam indicated a range of switches behind him. 'It's an offshoot of our mining research. Nuclear bombardment beams; we found our miners growing fur and claws . . . the better they thought to dig with.'

'Can the process be reversed?'

Quillam shrugged in reply to the Governor's enquiry.

'Who knows? We don't require such findings in the Punishment Dome.'

The Doctor decided to appeal to Quillam's vanity. 'You're a research scientist, a good one judged by the extent of the complex technology here and the novel engineering concepts of the Punishment Dome.'

'An experiment such as this has never been as advanced or as successful' Quillam boasted.

'Then try turning off the machine,' the Doctor urged. 'Their bodies might still revert to their former composition.'

Quillam shook his head and spoke with finality. 'Not possible, this research is vital for when I install new torture programmes into the Punishment Dome.'

Witnessing the scowling reaction of the Doctor the Governor tried one last tack.

'What if *I* insist, Mr Quillam?'

The masked scientist stiffened angrily and moved away from his controller chair. 'I have absolute authority here. I am the section master. No one orders me, certainly not a transient Governor.' Quillam paused then added in a tone laced with contempt, '*Sir.*'

The Governor took an impulsive step towards Quillam, the hostility flaring between them. All eyes were on the two antagonists; it was an opportunity that allowed Jondar to begin to ease away from the others and sidle towards Quillam's chair. Only the Doctor noticed Jondar's initiative and in order to allow Jondar more precious seconds stepped up alongside the Governor and asked Quillam abruptly, 'Do you still experiment on your own person?'

The masked face turned toward him. 'Not any more, why?'

103

'But in earlier days you placed yourself in much danger.'

'Yes. Why do you ask? How do you know?'

'Your mask . . .'

To everyone's surprise – and Quillam's astonishment – the Doctor audaciously reached forward and, before anyone could stop him, flicked apart the seal-strip that held the mask in place. The plastic cover fell away. For a second everyone stared, horrified, at the white scars, the riven cheekbones, the single wild staring eye bulging in a lidless socket. Everyone, that is, except Jondar who pounced on the security guard nearest to him and pulled the phaser from the surprised man's belt.

'Turn round,' he rapped out and while Quillam fumbled to replace his mask the Doctor quickly extracted the scientist's gun and covered the Varosians on the other side from Jondar who now levelled the weapon at Quillam threateningly. 'Turn off the transmutation process or die!'

With his face mask once more back in place Quillam became calm and more authoritative. 'Take your choice. There must be a thousand switches to pick from . . . if it *is* a switch that controls the bombardment beam.'

Bewilderment passed across Jondar's handsome face as he viewed the maze of instrumentation behind him.

'Doctor, can you decide which?' he asked in frustration.

'No time,' the Doctor said and levelled his phaser at what he guessed must be a transitional inductor panel and pressed the 'destroy' button. A bolt of sheer red force sped across the chamber, smashing into membranes of metal, delicate rotational systems and a kinetic energiser which exploded, showering the chamber with white hot steel fragments. 'Aim, Jondar, aim!' the Doctor yelled. Firing at random they emptied their phasers into the technological nerve centre, smashing some systems and crippling others; gambling and praying as they did so that one of these would be the circuit that fed the bombardment beam that had so distorted the bodies of Areta and Peri. Finally they left the smoke-filled chamber with its still fragmenting and burning circuitry and retreated, forcing a guard officer, Maldak, to go with them.

Left behind in the devastated control chamber the Governor and his party regrouped.

'After them!' he ordered the security guards. The men looked askance to Quillam but he paid no attention to their confused loyalty. Already he was calculating how long it would be before he could rebuild his beloved power base and once more control all the infernal machinery of the Punishment Dome.

Under threat of the depleted energy weapon Maldak showed the Doctor and Jondar the route through the rehabilitation centre towards the transmutation cell. Keys jangled, but at last he found the correct key and opened the door, allowing Jondar and the Doctor to be reunited with Areta and Peri – or what had been Areta and Peri. Now a large green lifeless lizard lay beside an unmoving grotesque vulture-like bird.

'What can we do, Doctor?' The Doctor pointed silently towards Maldak, sending him into a corner away from the door with a gesture; he wanted, needed, all his concentration. The process of refractive bombardment had at least ceased, but had life ceased for the two women also? Neither moved. Fearing the worst, the Doctor moved forward to examine the grotesque changelings who lay on the laboratory table.

13

Realm of Chaos

The Doctor bent over the large black bird that had been Peri and shook his head sadly. Beside him Jondar gently lifted the scaled green arm of Areta, searching for a pulse, however faint.

'Anything?' the Doctor asked.

Jondar sighed. 'Hard to tell. The skin is so thick, so . . . look!' The Doctor turned to where Jondar pointed. 'Peri . . . she . . . it . . . moved . . . and . . . yes, there's something here. A faint heartbeat. They're alive!' A movement in the corner of the cell distracted them. It was Maldak, making a dart for freedom. With a roar Jondar charged across the cell but the guard had the start on him and banged the door against his pursuer. The impact of the cell door sent Jondar sprawling which allowed Maldak to make his escape.

'Sorry . . .' groaned Jondar.

'No matter, not if we can move out quickly before they can locate us.'

'How?'

The Doctor had been examining the NBD above the two changelings. 'We might just have stopped the process before the transformation was complete. Without the final phase bombardment their bodily metabolism might possibly be reasserting itself. That's perhaps why you couldn't feel Areta's pulse at first . . . But if the scale is becoming thinner that would allow her pulse to become detectable.'

'Doctor – ' Jondar began impatiently.

'Yes . . . I know. We must move or be trapped here . . . you mentioned that there is supposed to be a safe exit somewhere.'

'On the other side of the Dome. But to reach it from here is impossible . . .'

The Doctor began to raise Peri from the table where Jondar had started to unbuckle the strapping that held Areta.

'The odds are now unpredictable,' the Doctor said as he helped the slowly reviving Peri to her feet. 'With the control centre damaged we might have an outside chance of getting through. We must move on. Come on Peri.' A croak of dazed response came from the throat of the black-feathered half-woman half-bird. 'Peri . . . you are Peri. You will change back . . . you must. Try. *Must* move!' The bird croaked again in reply to the Doctor's urgings. This time the sound could have been a rasping attempt to speak her name. The Doctor could not be certain but it could be that there seemed rather less feathers than had been there moments before.

'Doctor . . . I think Areta's changing back . . . slowly . . . her hands are almost clear . . . Areta! Areta!'

'We must leave . . .' the Doctor said.

'I can't, not without Areta,' Jondar protested.

'We must take them with us . . . Peri . . . can you hear, understand?'

The head of the bird moved up and down drowsily. A voice still rasping but just recognisable grated out: 'Who . . . am . . . I . .?'

'You are Peri. *Peri* . . !'

'Me . . . me . . . you . .?'

'I am the Doctor. We must find a way out. Now!'

Supporting the two women who had begun increasingly to revert back to their former selves, the Doctor and Jondar carried the still almost comatose pair out of

107

the cell and into the corridor to face the dangers that lay before them within the prison control sector and after that the unknown terrors of the Punishment Dome.

Trying hard to note the rapidly changing images flicking across her home screen, Etta finally gave up the battle and looked up from her viewstat report.

'I just don't understand what's happening.'

'Neither do they,' said Arak sourly, nodding at the screen. Stung by the criticism of the ruling class she served so loyally, Etta rallied to their defence. 'The videoers know what they are doing.'

'Then what's going on? Boring scenes of Punishment World for days. Now this. Rubbish. Drowning tanks filling and emptying with no prisoners inside. Rubbish. You'd watch anything.'

'No,' said Etta decisively, returning to her report determinedly. 'I wouldn't watch you.'

The main screen in Quillam's domain came back to life after non-stop feverish activity from his team of technicians. The picture showed a barrier of steel-tipped spears senselessly rising and falling somewhere in an ordeal sector on the outer rim of the Punishment Dome.

Quillam indicated the screen to the Chief who stood anxiously beside him. 'Some devices work, some are out of control, some will be out of action until we can manage a complete repair.'

'Why not shut off all the power?'

'And allow every prisoner in the Dome to escape? No. What of the Doctor and his companions?'

'I have every patrol out looking for him with orders to kill.'

'Good. The screens will continue to transmit pictures into the homes of Varos and to me here. It is the only way I can assess the damage done by the Doctor to my Punishment Dome.'

'But everyone on Varos can witness the confusion.'

'All they will see is spectacle . . . bizarre happenings, strange sights and think we have arranged them. All prisoners will be at extreme risk because some of the Punishment Zones will operate unfairly, killing the careful as well as the reckless. That should entertain the viewpop long enough to allow us to repair the destruction here and to enable me once more to assume control.'

The Chief looked after Quillam who had moved away to assist in the rewiring of a transitional electroniser and called, 'This Doctor must be eliminated, he smells the truth of things.'

Quillam turned, the working lights glazing his mask. 'The Dome will take care of him,' he said, his confidence rising as the damage to his beloved technology began to be repaired.

As the Doctor and Jondar helped Peri and Areta along a dusty disused passage they could hear in the distance sounds of unruly discord as the Punishment Dome sound system reacted to the damage done by the group who now had to cross this realm of chaos towards the mythical safe exit which allowed freedom and pardon for anyone fortunate enough to survive the rigours of Quillam's fiendish ingenuity.

Now, thought the Doctor grimly as he guided the still dazed Peri along, now the random factor of damaged computer systems might make their survival impossible. But there was no other option, the Doctor told himself as they maintained their slow progress towards where the sounds of disharmony grew even louder. This, the Doctor guessed, must be the area where the Punishment Dome and prison control merged. Soon their ordeal would begin in earnest. To survive they would need not only luck and ingenuity but as much strength as they could muster. Already it seemed an age since they had carried the two stupefied women away from the transmutation cell. The Doctor glanced back at Jondar.

'We'll rest here.'

Jondar and the Doctor eased Areta and Peri down so that they could rest against the hewn rock of the passage wall. The physical exertion of their escape and the constant exhortations of the Doctor and Jondar to remember their names and who they truly were had helped to change the two women back to almost a full resumption of their former appearance. Yet both remained dull and disorientated as they stared ahead, still hardly comprehending who they were or what danger they soon might have to face.

'Let's check the next opening,' the Doctor said, pointing. Jondar said nothing in reply but simply followed the Doctor towards the end of the passage.

On reaching the junction of corridors the Doctor pointed downwards indicating the patrol car monorail that ran past their corridor and disappeared into the distance. Almost simultaneously with the Doctor's gesture the monorail began to vibrate, indicating the approach of a vehicle and at the same time a video scan camera that covered the section of corridor glowed alertly. Evidently the communication systems were being given priority in restoring the efficiency of the Punishment Dome.

Stepping back out of sight before the camera could locate them, the Doctor and Jondar both waited, praying that the approaching patrol car would pass them by. The ominous swish of the car increased as it came closer and closer, passed, then slowed to a halt. Oh, no, the Doctor thought, someone had noticed their passageway and had decided to investigate.

Jondar eased his phaser energy weapon out and checked its charge reading. The dial registered low and would probably contain no more than a few feeble bolts at best. Setting the force to 'stun' might give half a dozen shots but it would hardly be enough to stem any serious attack. Still, there would be the element of initial surprise.

As if reading Jondar's thoughts, the Doctor pointed towards the stationary patrol car and began to flatten himself against the nearside passage wall, alert and ready to lay ambush. Jondar joined the Doctor, listening alertly for the sound of the guards' approach. Soon the noise of boots marching on the rocky floor was heard advancing nearer and nearer. Jondar lifted his phaser in readiness while the Doctor determined to do what he could to assist in repelling the advancing patrol. The half a dozen men were almost upon them when the Doctor realised with a tinge of hope that the marching steps were not slowing and that they might have a slim chance of remaining undiscovered. Hurriedly he put a restraining hand onto Jondar's shoulder. His upraised phaser weapon dropped slightly as the guards marched by without a glance into the gloom of the disused corridor where the fugitives sheltered.

Then disaster! 'Doctor!' a terrified voice that was undoubtedly Peri's rang out from behind them, halting the guards. Instantly Jondar acted, stepping out and firing at the patrol who scattered away in confusion. 'The car . . . we can take their car!' Jondar yelled in excitement, firing another precious bolt. 'I can cover you . . . Areta?'

Areta, recovered just enough to understand his call, came slowly forward to join him and the Doctor but

111

Peri, as soon as the first shot was fired, had set off in the other direction back down the dark corridor.

'Peri!' the Doctor yelled after her but she had disappeared before even the echo of his voice had called back to him.

'The car . . . we can find her later . . . Doctor, there is no choice . . . go, I'll cover you while I can!'

The Doctor realised Jondar was right. Hopefully they could circle round on the monorail and catch up with Peri. It was the best chance, for the guards had by now regrouped and the red bolts of their force phasers were beginning to sheer past them as the trio began to run for the empty patrol car.

A force bolt ricochetted from the shining black surface of the patrol car as the Doctor opened the door panel. Hastily he hauled Areta inside then swayed aside as Jondar scrambled in to join them. The car shuddered as a concentrated volley of phaser shots flared against the toughened steel.

Fumbling with the control panel, the Doctor pressed buttons and flicked switches without success but then clutched the steering column and squeezed a finger panel half-way down its length. The car jerked forward crazily then accelerated away from the running guards who fired wildly after their disappearing patrol car until it careered round a corner and went out of their sight.

'That's more like it!' Arak applauded the escape of the rebels on his home screen.

Etta referred back to her notes and frowned. 'I thought that rebo with the coat of coloured patches was to be executed.'

'No,' said Arak scornfully. 'He's escaped again. Do pay attention.' Then he smirked as a slight frown of worry appeared on his wife's brow. 'You'd better check your viewstat sheets again, love. Wouldn't do to make a false report or you'll be in the Punishment Dome with them.'

In the Governor's office a confrontation was taking place between the ruler of Varos and the being who coveted his position of power.

'My insulted parson – *correction – person* can stand no more. Either you sign the newly-agreed price for the Zeiton ore or I will leave you and these Varosian persons to starve on this miserablest of planets with nothing to eat but unsold Zeitony!'

The Governor seemed unimpressed by Sil's bluster. 'I must know more . . .' he began but before he could finish the door to his office opened and a bewildered girl was pushed into the office by two guards. 'Peri . . .'

'Found wandering near Prison Control,' the Chief announced entering after his men. There was something different about the tone of the Chief Officer's voice that to the Governor's sense of danger sounded like a warning. 'I brought her here to display as evidence before the people.'

'I will decide when and if I broadcast, Chief.'

The Chief drew from his holster a phaser weapon and trained it on the Governor. 'Not any more. The regulations have a clause for just the situation that we are in now. At the end of each Governor's term there comes a time of disapproval when the people finally tire of his incompetence. The only wish of viewpop then is to vote him down.'

'To see all the cells of his body destroyed!' Sil interjected delightedly.

'When that final vote is being avoided, as I believe it is now, the Chief Officer is empowered to insist on a final vote. Governor, you have to accept responsibility for failing to quell the prison rebellion led by this woman, Peri, and her companion, the one they call the Doctor!'

113

The Chief glanced at the guards. Two more phasers appeared to threaten the Governor and Peri. The Chief smiled, his thick lips stretching into a mocking grimace.

'Prepare for your final broadcast, Governor,' the Chief ordered, while in the background Sil clapped his tiny green hands together in wild applause at the prospect of the Governor's final fall.

14

The Final Vote

The Governor slumped wearily into the chair that soon would hold him in its grasp and not release him until the annihilation process was complete. Peri stood near him, trying to clear her mind of the last lingering traces of her own transmutation ordeal. Across the room one silent guard, Maldak, stayed watching them, his hand never far away from the open holster that contained his phaser gun.

'Here we will die as have so many Governors . . .'

Peri assumed the 'we' meant the Governor was using it the way royalty sometimes did. At least she hoped that was the case.

'The Chief will claim his right to broadcast first; anything I say after that will sound like so much bluster,' the Governor continued.

'Let me speak . . .' pleaded Peri. 'Tell the people what I've just told you – the truth.'

The Governor sighed. 'Ramblings of someone deranged by the transmogrification process, that's what they will say. I believe you now. Now that it is all too late . . .'

Peri stamped a petulant foot at the defeatism in his voice and insisted fiercely, 'But I'm all right now!'

The Governor looked away. 'We haven't a hope, Peri.'

The leader's gloom deflated Peri a little but she tried to imagine what the Doctor would do and began glancing around the office, searching for a way out.

'How long have we got?' she demanded.

'Not long. Once the officer elite is assembled the twelve most senior officers must gather to witness a final vote-down . . . once the Governor is eliminated regulations insist the dozen candidates place their names in hazard. The unlucky winner is brought in here and forced to govern.'

'And to go through the same daft process you did?'

'Yes.' A mirthless smile formed on the Governor's mouth. 'The theory being that a man terrified for his life will somehow find solutions to this planet's problems. The poor unfortunate will discover, like me, that there are no popular solutions to the difficulties he will find waiting for him here.'

'That's crazy! Cruel!'

'It's Varos,' the Governor said flatly and stood up and walked across to the guard who straightened nervously at his leader's approach. The Governor studied the guard carefully.

'Maldak, isn't it?'

'Yes, sir.'

'Put your gun down, Maldak, I've no intention of trying to escape.'

'Can't do that, sir.'

'Maldak, weren't you elected to the officer corps when my name was drawn as Governor?'

'Correct, sir,' said Maldak stiffly, wondering where all this might be leading him.

'Might I ask one favour, Maldak? Let this girl go free. You know what will happen. She could easily slip away while all eyes are on my destruction.'

'Can't do that, sir,' Maldak said again uncertainly.

'You know that once I am dead a new Governor must be elected?'

'That is the custom, yes, sir.'

'What if the name they draw is yours, Maldak?' The

116

Governor watched Maldak's expression for the slightest tremor of doubt but the guard looked stolidly back at him. It was hopeless, the Governor thought bitterly, Varosians were a servile race, even this man who was almost one of the elite. It was a futile attempt, he realised, but he continued anyway.

'You have witnessed how impossible the system is, Maldak. You are an intelligent man. The regulations are archaic, distorted, unworkable . . . even if you escape drawing the red counter you will suffer once an enquiry is called. New Governors always hold enquiries, don't they, Maldak? The enquiry will establish that you showed the Doctor and the rebel Jondar where the women were being transmuted.'

'Couldn't help that, sir!' Maldak burst out. 'They had a phaser at my head.'

'They'll say you should have resisted.' Emotion showed on Maldak's face for the first time since the Governor had begun addressing him. What was it? Fear? Perhaps. The Governor decided to add his final card to this last finesse for freedom.

'I wonder what execution ritual they will star you in, Maldak? Something spectacular to mark the new Governor's term of office. I hope you enjoy the experience.' The Governor turned away, shaking his head for effect and had gone several steps before Maldak's uncertain voice called after him.

'What do you think I should do, sir?'

The Governor turned eagerly, too eagerly. He cursed his impatience for the guard, trained since birth to obey orders, was already struggling against the momentary disloyalty, and the Governor's sudden enthusiastic move back towards him betrayed his unease at refusing to follow the ritualistic regulations stoically.

Both men looked at each other for a long moment, centuries of tradition and obedience to regulation struggling within them. Finally Peri could stand the silence no longer.

'Let us go, Maldak . . .' she begged. 'Come with us. We can find the Doctor, he knows much more than I do. He'll tell you what is really going on here!'

'I can't disobey my orders . . .'

'Perhaps not for my sake, but Peri is innocent,' said the Governor.

'No, sir . . . Sorry.'

The Governor tried to rescue an iota of advantage. 'After the vote goes against me please do one thing . . . kill Peri to spare her from Quillam and the rehabilitators.'

Maldak looked away from them both, unable to meet their eyes, unable to make even this last refusal vocal. So be it, the Governor thought resignedly.

'I tried . . .' he said gently to Peri, then took her hand and looked down at her.

'We will die together,' he said simply and began to lead her towards his desk and the waiting chair.

The patrol car in which the Doctor, Jondar and Areta were travelling came to a meeting of corridors. Now able to drive with some degree of control the Doctor slowed the car and brought it to a fairly smooth halt. The trio climbed out and each took a passageway stepping along for some way and calling out Peri's name. No reply came. Rejoining the others the Doctor climbed back into the driving seat. He was almost certain that they had covered every metre of the area Peri could have reached by now. Nor could he understand why their progress had been unimpeded by pursuers. He sensed that something else must be going on that was occupying the authorities' attention. He wondered what that might be and hoped against hope that it did not involve Peri.

*　　*　　*

Arak and Etta stared, absorbed, at their wall screen. A final vote-down was always an exciting event. In big close-up the Chief Officer was completing his summary of the Governor's shortcomings and reasons for the final vote-in. Leaning forward to the camera the moist plump lips forced out the last drop of feigned sincerity.

'This is a forced vote. I have explained my actions. The Governor must now explain his. After which, you, my fellow Varosians, must use your votes and resolve the matter finally.'

The fleshy lips parted into an uneven smile of complete confidence at the outcome of his request.

'It's useless. She's gone or been captured.' Areta voiced all their thoughts as they sat in the patrol car after another fruitless search.

'Perhaps.' The Doctor hated giving up but prison control was silent, empty. Even the cameras were no longer glowing with their dull red glow. The Doctor tried the finger panel and nothing happened. 'No power. They've turned the supply off . . .'

'Deliberately?'

'Maybe for repair . . . or to isolate us . . . or maybe they need the power for something else.'

'A Governor's vote-down.' Areta and Jondar stared at each other. Jondar opened the door but sat unmoving.

'I think they've got Peri. They'll get us too unless we move into the Punishment Dome before they can get it working properly again.'

'Could we find the hidden exit?' Areta asked, expecting the usual scorn about the impossibility of the feat from Jondar.

'We can try,' Jondar said surprisingly and swung his legs down and stood up, stretching his arms up above his head and staring defiantly down the darkened corridor that led into unknown danger.

Areta turned to the Doctor. 'Come with us. We need you.'

'All right,' the Doctor said. There was nothing else he could say or do.

Listening to the Governor's reply to the Chief Arak jumped as the instruction 'Vote! Vote' started to flash across his home screen and across the Governor's image.

'That's not right!' Etta exclaimed. 'The Governor hasn't finished speaking yet!'

On screen the Governor smiled sadly. Behind him, Peri could be seen, a forlorn figure who had done her best to support the Governor's arguments and, to Arak, laughable assertion that Zeiton-7 might be a precious commodity.

'I am not afraid to die,' the Governor concluded.

'Good!' said Arak and stood up and reached for the "No" button on his wall panel. Pressing his vote was not enough for the excited Arak. So anxious was he to vote the Governor down that he impulsively used Etta's 'No' vote in addition to his own.

'Hey!' said Etta indignantly but it was too late. Arak's vote on her behalf against the beleagured Governor had already been added to the growing total against his survival.

'No!' Peri screamed as the restraining clamps activated and held the Governor captive in his chair indicating that the negative votes had reached a majority. Red and green beams of debilitation came pouring down upon the hapless Governor who gamely continued his appeal to the cameras.

'Our system is wrong, we sell ourselves for nothing to such as Sil and his like . . . Ah!' The beams intensified their force as if trying to still the Governor's tongue. Groaning, the Governor began to suffer so much that his last words were gasped out with his remaining resources of strength. 'I see my . . . my . . . words mean nothing. That you all wish the harsh system to continue . . . so . . . be . . . it . . .'

Across the room Maldak had taken his phaser from his holster and was levelling it at Peri. Thinking he was about to give her a merciful release through death didn't make it any easier to bear. 'No, please, no!' Peri shouted but the guard's finger tightened and the deadly beam seared towards her. Peri closed her eyes and waited for burning destruction to strike, but instead the bolt hit where it had been aimed – at the power cable that fed the HCD device that had been pouring destruction down upon the Governor. As the cable melted the power supply suddenly ceased, allowing the Governor to free his arms with a last feeble effort.

Etta saw the Governor's dramatic escape from death and turned upon her husband accusingly. 'See what you've done, Arak. You've messed up the whole system by voting twice. They'll be coming round for you . . . using someone else's vote is forbidden! It's a serious criminal offence,' she added gloatingly as her man stared at the screen which showed the Governor being helped out of his chair by Peri and his rescuer, Maldak.

'I didn't do all that though, did I?' said Arak, trembling at the thoughts that followed his wife's words.

In the prison control centre Quillam and Sil turned from their screen and angrily remonstrated with the crestfallen Chief Officer.

'What incompetence has overtook us now!' Sil shrilled out hysterically. 'Why can't people simply get killed anymore!'

*   *   *

'Hurry, sir,' Maldak urged his exhausted leader. 'Soon the other guards will break in.'

'Where can we, where should we go?'

'We must join the Doctor,' Peri said, but then remembered, 'If we knew where he was.'

'There was a report that they were heading for the End Zone. We were told to concentrate on getting rid of the Governor then to go and get the Doctor once and for all.'

'I'm glad you changed your mind, Maldak,' the Governor said, painfully gasping with the effort. 'The Doctor must be seeking the safe exit.'

'Let's go there then!' Peri urged. Maldak didn't reply but opened a side door at the rear of the office and checked that their escape was possible. Obviously it was for he waved them through.

Concentrating hard, the Governor outlined his plan. 'We could try and get into the Punishment Dome from the outside. It should be easy to locate the safe exit location . . . go in . . . find the Doctor . . . join forces.'

'The outside, sir. I've never been . . .'

'I know where there are protective suits. What I say must be attempted. From now on there'll be no more ritualised formalities of death. Should we be caught we will be gunned down instantly as will the Doctor!'

15

Into the End Zone

The power had been restored to the Punishment Dome as soon as the vote-in had been completed and the depleted energy system repaired. As the cameras reactivated and began once more to monitor their progress, Jondar voiced all their thoughts. 'I wonder why we have been allowed to travel this far into the Dome without being apprehended?'

'Maybe the whole place is cracking up. The guards might be as confused as we are,' Areta suggested.

Jondar shook his head in disbelief. They walked on for a moment then he shared a further worry. 'I think we are into what they call the End Game. Very few trialists ever reach this stage.'

Walking a few paces behind them, the Doctor had been listening thoughtfully. 'Would that be where this mythical safe exit might be?'

'Presumably.'

'Hm . . .' said the Doctor. 'That's probably why they haven't bothered to chase us. If it's the final furlong there's probably something particularly nasty waiting that they think will see us all off.'

'Maybe,' said Jondar.

'Anyhow,' the Doctor said cheerfully, 'we had better be cautious . . . the mind games and jolly little tricks lie behind us that's for certain.'

Jondar nodded his agreement. 'What we are entering now is known as the area of most dangerous ordeal . . .'

As if someone or something had been eavesdropping on their conversation a rumble of gloating laughter began to be heard above them and grew in volume as they advanced along the passageway. All exchanged wary glances. The End Game had begun.

'You are incompetent profitless fools!' Sil glared at Quillam and the Chief Officer malevolently. 'The Governor and the girl have escaped. Your viewers are laughing at you. I think you have lost your tower – *correction* – *power*!'

'That is not true.' The Chief pointed at two open-topped patrol cars full of armed troops and guards. 'I still control the forces of order.'

'Not for much longing!' spat Sil. 'This Doctor meets up with the Governor and tells him the truth of your treachery over all these yearlings, you will be in the hot seat for good.'

'He is right,' said Quillam quietly.

'This time . . .' the Chief began to bluster.

'This time,' Quillam insisted, 'I will lead the search for them personally.'

'That is not your province,' the Chief began then changed his tack abruptly. 'You may come along, Mr Quillam but *I* will lead.'

Quillam did not bother to reply but climbed purposefully into the front seat of the leading patrol car. Not to be outdone, the Chief pushed in beside him and pointed forward. 'Let's find and destroy these rebels,' he ordered pompously.

The patrol cars packed to the doors with militia began to glide away, much to Sil's secret delight. When he was left alone with his attendants he fleefully and openly boasted about the ploy he had just successfully achieved. 'Fools! While they rush around after the Doctor, I will be welcoming our invasion force. Varos and all its wealth will soon be ours – or better still, mine! The mines will be all mine!' It was not a wonderful pun but to Sil it was a scintillating witticism that sent him into surges of gurgling delight.

A silver mist had slowly filled the corridor surrounding the Doctor and the others. The gloating deep ghostly laughter increased as the eerie silver mist enshrouded them, then, softly, the enticing music began. Based on the whale music of far-off earth the Doctor realised that it was having a hypnotic effect on Jondar and Areta who seemed entranced by its seductive dreamlike quality. Smiling, they wandered on into the enfolding silvery atmosphere as the laughter deepened and surrounded them.

'Stop!' a command issued from above in godlike tones. Obediently all three stopped then watched curiously as their shadows left them and moved on ahead then, inexplicably the black wraiths turned to their former owners and beckoned them forward.

Jondar and Areta obediently followed; only the Doctor resisted the strange command, puzzled as to why the invitation should be necessary. Then realisation dawned.

'No! Begone!' he yelled out with all the force his lungs could muster. 'I am real, you are but shadows . . . ghosts . . . insubstantial! *We* exist; you do not!'

Pointing at each of the three black silhouettes in turn the Doctor's will exerted itself and slowly each shadow dematerialised as the mist cleared, leaving the three of them standing on the edge of a seething pit of fire from which they had been but a step away.

Taking a deep breath of relief the Doctor looked enquiringly at Areta and Jondar. 'Should we try another route?'

'Yes, please,' said Areta stepping back from the flames with some alacrity.

*   *   *

Outside on the harsh surface world of Varos a sharp wind blew against the exterior of the Punishment Dome. Peri was glad that the Governor had foreseen the need for protective clothing as well as breathing equipment to allow them to move along the pitted outerside of the Dome. Placed between the two men, in her black shiny protective suit, Peri could feel the impact of the red grit driven by the constant gale. Communication between all three was impossible except through gesture. Leading the way, the Governor went on, blindly seeking the doorway into the Dome that contained the Doctor.

The body lay sprawled across the full width of the corridor. Such was the extent of the dangers already survived that the Doctor and his two companions all suspected a trap of some sort. Warily they approached the inert body. It was obviously that of a prisoner, judging by the ragged clothes and begrimed hands. The dead man's face remained hidden by an arm flung protectively across as if his last wish had been to hide from the scrutiny of the camera that hovered above.

'Who would he be?' the Doctor asked.

Jondar shrugged. 'Maybe someone who was condemned and survived this far. Maybe one of the residents . . .'

'Residents?'

'Wretches who are relatives of the condemned without anyone to support them. They come into the Dome with their breadwinners. After their loved one dies they survive somehow.' Areta looked down at the dead man. 'Don't ask me how.'

The Doctor bent down to examine the corpse and moved the arm away from the dead man's face. The skin was blue and the expression shocking with the bulging eyes frozen in terror.

126

Areta turned away. 'What could have done that?'

The Doctor opened the grimy collar of the ragged grey prison shirt. 'That's what killed him . . .' The others looked at where the Doctor was pointing. A purple contusion formed a ring on the neck. Inside the circle was a small series of incisions as if inflicted by a sucker of some sort. 'His neck seems swollen as if to burst. Poison?'

Jondar glanced around the bare rock walls about them. 'Poison that he'd taken or had been given?'

A theory began to form in the Doctor's mind. 'Maybe neither . . .' he began but before the sequence of thought could complete itself a cry from Areta diverted all his attention.

'Doctor!' The terrified cry turned the Doctor and Jondar away from the poisoned body. Creeping towards them slavering and growling like hungry animals were a large pack of residents. Then Jondar did an astonishing thing by stepping towards the mob.

'Friends . . .' he began before the Doctor quite realised what he was contemplating. Hurriedly, taking Jondar's arm firmly, the Doctor turned him about.

'No speeches, Jondar, please.'

For a moment they stood their ground and watched the red-eyed, slavering mob edging towards them. Areta trembled. 'What should we do, Doctor?'

'Run,' said the Doctor calmly. Then turned and together with Areta and Jondar ran just as fast as they possibly could with the crowd of howling screaming wretches chasing them.

On the airless exterior of the Dome the Governor's exploring fumbling gloved hand touched metal rather than the pitted plastic that he had been searching his way along for the past hour.

Wiping their visors clear of the red shale, they examined the shape of a protruding handle. The rest of the door was hidden by layers of red shale driven against the Dome by the surface wind. Pointing, the Governor began to clear away the caked layers of grit. Maldak and Peri joined him.

Peri thought grimly of the final deceit that this final 'safe' exit represented. Any prisoner who found his way here from inside would step directly out into an airless world which would cause them instant death without breathing apparatus. What despicable creatures the Varosian rulers were!

Inside her helmet, Peri frowned with a determination that promised vengeance on the ruling elite for all the lives broken within the dome of despair they were about to try and enter.

The rim of the door was now almost fully visible and free of sand. The Governor pulled on the level. Nothing happened. Then Maldak lent his weight to the task and very stiffly the level dropped perhaps an inch. Both men pulled with all their strength and slowly the handle moved, fully allowing them to slide open the door.

Ducking inside they found themselves entering an airlock with another, inner door that would not open until the outer door was sealed. Slowly the air pressure equalised itself and the inner door opened. The Governor, Peri and Maldak cautiously stepped inside an area of the Dome that seemed strangely humid. Soon they felt the need to discard their helmets and protective clothing.

'Why is it so hot?' Peri asked.

'I don't know . . .' said the Governor, wiping perspiration from his forehead. 'This section was designed before my time. Let's find out, shall we?' Having come this far, there was nothing else to do. In jungle-like heat the rescuers began to walk down a ramp that led into the mysterious End Zone.

*   *   *

Eventually, the superior fitness of the Doctor's party began to overcome the desperate initial rush of the crazed mob chasing them. 'What do they want . . ?' gasped Areta as the distance between them and their pursuers gradually increased.

'Who knows?' Jondar panted as they turned a corner where a blast of warm almost tropical air greeted them.

'Keep running!' the Doctor ordered and the trio did so, perspiring profusely in the increasingly humid atmosphere.

'Faster!' the Chief ordered his driver urgently as the patrol car zoomed forward ever deeper into the Punishment Dome.

'Ah!' said Arak who had been grumbling at the lack of action on his home screen. He had mastered the apprehension at the prospect of what he imagined would be an imminent visit from Pol Corps. He had decided that his wife had been persecuting him about his transgression over the purloined vote and now he was settled in front of his home screen awaiting some entertainment.

Etta entered and pushed a plate of essence of sandmole before Arak who reached for it and transferred it to his mouth automatically.

'What's been happening?' Etta indicated the screen.

'Hard to tell. There's lots of shots of two patrol cars speeding along. A group of residents charging about – and hey, look, it's that guy in the patchwork coat. They're after him.'

'Great. I like him . . . there's always action when he's on screen.'

Then the peculiar taste of the sand mole distorted Arak's taste buds and he grimaced but forced the protein ration down his protesting gullet manfully. 'Yeh.

Very nice.' he lied, glad to concentrate on the chase between the Doctor and the residents once more.

There was now some fifty metres between the Doctor and his companions and the pursuing residents. Ahead of them was what seemed to be a jungle of luxuriant green foliage with water and a growth of hanging creepers whose purple fronds trailed down almost to within a few metres of the undergrowth.

The heat was intense and seeing the sparkling gleam and hearing the sound of a small waterfall made Areta quicken her stride and pull ahead of the Doctor and Jondar hoping to gain time for a mouthful of water.

Purple fronds, the Doctor thought, then realised the danger.

'Areta, if you value your life don't touch those tendrils!'

Uncertainly Areta stopped on the far edge of the jungle clearing where the trailing creepers began. The mob of residents by this time were gaining ground on the faltering Doctor and Jondar who had no option but to join Areta.

'Into the vines . . . but careful . . . we mustn't allow a single touch!'

Ultra-carefully the Doctor led the way, slowly man-oeuvering into the forest of deadly creepers. The mob came nearer but also slowly and very cautiously. The slow chase became one of painstakingly meticulous progress.

'What do they want with us?' Areta asked again as the leading wretch advanced through the hanging vines. So close was he now that she could smell his foul breath and see the saliva drooling from his cracked lips as he closed in on her. Then her adversary blundered by reaching for her a second too soon. A tendril brushed his outstretched arm, another his jugular vein. The effect was terrifyingly instantaneous. A howl of agony came from the unfortunate man who convulsed then fell into a state of paralysis as the venom of the vine journeyed through his bloodstream.

The Doctor and the others stood horrified as the reason for their being hunted by the pack of residents became apparent: the mob were pulling their stricken comrade clear with every intention of satisfying their hunger in a disgusting and gruesome way.

'Cannibals,' Areta said faintly and swayed, almost coming into contact with a baneful creeper herself.

Jondar steadied her as, at that moment, through the hanging vines they saw the two patrol cars hurtling into view, their protective covering down to allow the guards to fire at the mob of feasting residents.

'There they are!' yelled the Chief impetuously as he spied the Doctor and the others standing immobile amidst the poison forest. 'Charge! Kill!' he yelled. In the excitement only Quillam realised the danger as the cars drove forward; but it was too late to stop their impetus. With a roar the crowded vehicles bore into the deadly poison-laden creepers. The hanging fronds brushed all below them in the passing cars and soon did their deadly work. Within minutes the cruel rulers of Varos were just so many grotesque puppets scattered and frozen in attitudes of surprised death within their silent stationary patrol cars.

The Doctor turned away. Already he could see more hungry residents arriving, moving stealthily through the vines towards the patrol cars, anxious for a free lunch.

'Let's move on but carefully, *very* carefully,' the Doctor said quietly.

Turning their backs on the fallen rulers and the mob now wreaking a terrible revenge, the Doctor led Areta and Jondar deeper into the deadly jungle.

*   *   *

On the other side of the treacherous disorder of poison vines, Peri, the Governor and Maldak had paused uncertainly on coming to the unexpected sprouting of tropical greenery.

'Phew!' Peri couldn't help exclaiming as she pulled her sweat stained shirt away from the hollow of her back. 'This is out of a book by Edgar Rice Burroughs.'

'What?' said the Governor, not understanding.

'Nothing. A writer, that's all.'

'There's no other way forward,' Maldak pronounced. 'It's either back to the safe exit or on through this – what's the word?'

'Jungle,' said Peri. Seeing the deep greens and purple vines excited her. It seemed so long since she had seen anything like foliage. It reminded her of Earth and its tropical regions.

'Let me lead,' she said. 'I always wanted to play Jane in a Tarzan picture! Never mind.' she added before the Governor could ask what on Earth she meant. 'Let's go . . .'

The Governor exchanged wry glances of incomprehension with Maldak as they began to follow the eager Peri into the forest with its straggling purple creepers.

Suddenly a familiar voice boomed out: 'Stop! Stay exactly where you are!'

The surprise of the command was enough to halt Peri just before she was about to push her way through the hanging tendrils.

'Doctor?' she called.

'The vines are filled with poison. Don't move until we reach you!'

'Wha – what!' gulped Peri, staring fascinated at the purple fronds that on closer view contained hundreds of miniscule suckers just waiting to disgorge their deadly toxin into the unwary.

Through the trailing creepers the outline of a bulky

figure began to become visible. Very slowly the Doctor advanced, swaying this way and that, carefully, so very carefully, until he emerged safely to be reunited with Peri in the safe haven that lay between the last ordeal of the End Zone and the one 'safe' exit that led out of the Punishment Dome.

'Are we safe? Is it over?' Peri sobbed with relief into the Doctor's shoulder.

'Yes it is,' another firm voice said. It belonged to the Governor who was helping Areta and Jondar to emerge unscathed from their last encounter with the horrors of the Punishment Dome.

'What are those vine things, Doctor?' The Doctor looked down at his companion. 'A Varosian version of rhus toxicodendron.'

'Poison ivy?'

There seemed no point in describing the havoc the deadly bane had wrought upon the controllers of Varos so the Doctor simply said, 'A bit like poison ivy, yes. Best to avoid contact if you can.'

'Don't worry, Doctor. Anything to do with Varos definitely goes into that category.'

'I'm sorry to hear that,' the Governor spoke softly. 'I would welcome your guidance in the establishment of a more libertarian system for Varos, Peri.'

The Doctor's companion's mind raced for a quick reply. 'Sorry, the Doc needs me . . . don't you, Doctor?' Peri swivelled and lifted her heel to give the Doctor a sharp and urgent reminder of her value.

'Oh . . . oh . . . yes . . . can't do without her . . . though I'm sure Peri would say that too rigid a system is often the antithesis of liberty. Wouldn't you, Peri?'

'Yeh, sure I would if I knew what it meant, Doctor.'

Then they laughed together. After a moment Areta joined them, then Jondar followed by Maldak; finally the Governor too managed a chuckle that said more for the future of Varos than any solemn vow ever could.

Goodbye to Varos

Sil, while waiting in his starship for the arrival of the invasion force from Thoros-Beta, was preening himself before a mirror held by an attendant. 'Mmm . . . lovely . . . lovely . . . I must look my very best when I take over this planet! How lovely am I? Very, very. Yes, I am . . . yes. Where are they? I must protest at this delay . . .'

Stabbing into a relay communications keyboard he spelled out: *Where is invasion fleet?*

After a moment, on the display screen above, came the cryptic reply: *Request denied. Your suspension apparent. Return to Thoros-Beta immediately!*

'What! Fools on the executive council have no nerve. We will ignore their insult of a summons home and take our skills to work for Amorb or anyone else who will dare to struggle to obtain total profit!'

So irate was the little green creature that all present in the cabin failed to notice a door slide open silently behind them.

'Prepare the ship, we blast off immediately!'

'I think not, Sil . . .' the Governor said quietly as he stood aside to allow his armed guards in to take control of the Thoros-Betan starship.

'How dare – ' Sil started.

'I have been in contact with your leader, Lord Kiv,' said the Governor. 'He is to send another negotiator to bargain a fair price for our valuable, our *most* valuable commodity of Zeiton-7.'

134

'What about *me*?' Sil wailed.

'You are to appear before Lord Kiv personally, it seems.'

The Governor, when he recounted the incident later, swore that Sil's green colouring lightened several shades at the prospect of such a meeting. Certainly from then on Sil caused no further trouble and had merely skulked in his water tank until another ship had arrived to whisk him back to the far-off watery planet of Thoros-Beta, there to try and use his wits and considerable guile to explain away his first commercial failure to the one creature he feared and respected – the mighty Lord Kiv.

In the days that had followed the destruction of the officer guard many changes had been promised for Varos, the most disturbing of which was the end of the compulsory video viewing of transmissions from within the Punishment Zone.

Arak and Etta sat dumbly before the screen as the Governor finished outlining his hopes and dreams for a free prosperous Varos. The familiar smile broadened on screen.

'My fellow Varosians, as you know from now on compulsory viewing is no longer required. You may do as you wish, watch what you wish.' The Governor chuckled. 'Even turn me off the screen now, if you so wish . . .' The Governor's image smiled, then faded. The familiar logo of Varos appeared with the national anthem playing quietly behind.

'Dare we try it,' asked Etta timidly.

'No more executions . . . nothing?' said Arak, nervously suspecting a trick.

'It's all changed. We're free . . . Whatever that is . . .' said Etta uncertainly. Then she reached for the control switch but her nerve failed her. 'I . . . I can't . . .'

'Let me,' Arak said bravely and tremblingly pressed the 'Off' button. The logo image collapsed into a tiny bright star that too began to fade. For a full minute man and wife gazed at the blank dull grey wall screen.

'What should we do?' Arak asked his wife finally.

'Don't know.'

Then, as one, they turned away from the empty wall and looked at each other, wonderingly.

The goodbyes had been said outside to the Governor and Maldak, to Areta and Jondar. Now Peri and the Doctor were alone once more inside the TARDIS. Wiping his hands after completing a final check on the completed repairs on the console before him, the Doctor said, 'The orthogenal readings haven't altered . . . Yes . . . Yes . . . everything's as it should be . . . the new elements and linings on the orbital transmission? Yes. Hunky-dory. We have your friend the Governor to thank for his most generous supply of Zeiton-7. Still, it's thanks to us that all Varos now knows their gift is more precious than gold.'

The Doctor became aware of a strangely silent and subdued Peri. 'Do you feel all right?' he enquired.

Peri had been remembering how traumatic the transmogrification process had been and now that they were preparing for flight through time this had recalled for her what it had been like to possess wings instead of arms.

'Are you sure you are all right?' the Doctor asked again.

'Apart from the residual side-effects of fowl pest, I feel great.'

'Just stay away from the millet and cuttle fish sandwiches then,' the Doctor joked.

'You're sure the TARDIS will function properly?' Peri asked anxiously.

'Oh, yes. We can leave at anytime we like. Disappointed?'

Peri shuddered at the thought of remaining on Varos. 'You think I'm crazy?'

'No . . .' said the Doctor, activating the dematerialisation mode successfully and watching the driving column begin to rise. 'Anyone who is as determined as you obviously are to leave a planet like Varos is very far from being crazy.'

In the old prison control centre the Governor, flanked by his new ministers and advisors watched, amazed, as the old-fashioned police box shimmered, faded then roared a final farewell to Varos and a people about to enjoy a new dawn.